VANISHED

by Hank Barone

ALSO BY HANK BARONE

HUNTED: In the footsteps of the Ancients

VANISHED

by Hank Barone

VANISHED

This book is a work of fiction. References to real
people, events, establishments, organizations or
locales are intended only to provide a sense of
authenticity, and are use fictitiously. All other
characters, and all incidents and dialogue, are drawn
from the author's imagination and are not construed
as real.

ISBN 978-0-578-08410-7

Published and distributed in the United States by:
International Media Group.

Cover design by Brooke Halladay
Cover photograph courtesy Ged Caddick/Terra
Incognita ECOTOURS (www.ecotours.com)

Dedication

For Joni, Kyle and Kelsey

Acknowledgements

With appreciation to Loran Foresman for sharing so many youthful adventures with me. And to Dimitar Krustev whose exciting trip to live with the Lacandon Indians in the jungles of Chiapas, Mexico, inspired me to write this novel. Also, to my wife Ellen, for her constant support and editing skills. A special thanks to my online critique group, Critsinternational.

1

Kidnappers would board Jake Brandon's bus in four minutes.

* * *

All six feet one of Jake Brandon, wearing ratty old Levis and a faded sky blue shirt, folded like an accordion into the cramped bus seat. He cursed his height as he angled his clunky hiking boots into the aisle of the crowded bus.

A young mother sat beside him in the window seat, her tiny baby wrapped in a blanket despite the day's heat. The young woman sang softly to her baby. Everywhere, passengers laughed and called to each other.

Ranchera music blasted from crackling speakers. A few men, drinking Carta Blanca beer from the bottle, sat in the back of the second-class bus.

The ancient bus creaked and swayed on the curvy mountain highway. Jake's seat mate touched his shoulder and, without a thought, handed him her baby. Jake cradled the infant, half afraid he'd drop it.

Reaching into the overhead bin, she dragged her backpack down. It brushed Jake's head.

"Lo siento, señor."

Seated again, she fumbled in her pack and pulled out a brown bag lunch. Taking back her baby, she offered Jake a burrito.

"Gracias, pero no."

The bus careened around a curve high above a jungle river, pushing Jake toward the young woman and the window. His stomach lurched as the bus leaned out over the drop-off, hugging the road's edge.

Jeez, no guardrails.

He braced himself as he stared down the rocky slope.

The driver hit the brakes. Jake's chin snapped down to his chest.

Jerking his head up, Jake grabbed the seat in front of him as he pitched forward.

The brakes screeched and the bus's backend swung toward the abyss as the driver wrestled the front toward the road's center.

Uh, oh. What's happening?

A battered army truck squatted across the two-lane highway. Five rifle-armed thugs in faded camouflage fatigues and ski masks stood shoulder to shoulder in front of the truck. Jake's sweaty hand slipped from the seat's back.

A husky bandit aimed his rifle at the driver. The music stopped.

The bus ground to a halt ten yards from the highwaymen.

No one spoke. A minute before the bus had sounded like a party. Now, it was as quiet as a funeral. The girl hugged her baby closer. Jake touched her arm.

This is going from a happy day, to possibly the worst day of my life.

The masked men strode toward the bus. One motioned the driver to open up as he continued to point his rifle at the man's head. The hydraulic door opened with an eerie hiss.

The lead highjacker, a dark skinned Indian, climbed the stairs, rifle ready. Two others followed.

The young mother scrunched down in her seat and shushed her baby. Jake held his breath.

The man paused at the top of the steps. His searching gaze settled on Jake, the only non-Mexican on the bus. Jake kept a poker face, but his stomach churned like a cement mixer. He gripped his hands hard to stop the trembling. Jake had heard about kidnappings and robberies, but never expected to be the victim of one. He rubbed his sweaty palms on his jeans.

The man strutted straight for him and thrust his left hand in front of Jake.

"Dame los documentos." He pointed the rifle at Jake's face. His dark brown eyes blazed through the ski mask's eye slits and his pinched, thin-lipped mouth barely moved through the mouth hole.

While Jake handed the man his papers, his gaze fixed on the gaping bore of the rifle's barrel, only inches away. His heart thudded against his chest so hard he thought it would burst.

The bandit ripped out Jake's iPod ear buds and grabbed a fistful of shirt. He yanked Jake to his feet and propelled him staggering toward the door. His sidekick shoved Jake to the top of the steps.

As the leader's powerful arms had jerked him to his feet, it sent chills down his spine. He'd been afraid lots of times and that had never stopped him. But this was a little more serious than fighting the school bully who had terrorized his best friend.

Halfway down the steps, the cold gun barrel pressed against the back of Jake's head brought home the danger he was in. The cords of his neck throbbed. The barrel jabbed into him, producing sharp pain, but anger, too.

This is crazy. I won't go peacefully. It's better to act now than wait.

Jake had recently won a New Mexico state wrestling championship. He hoped that the discipline he'd learned and the strength he'd gained from training year-round would help him now.

The roadway's hot surface burned through his hiking shoes. He stopped, ready.

The two remaining bandits stood beside the truck smoking and laughing. They paid no attention to Jake and his captor.

The rifle poked him forward.

Now. Act now. Jake willed himself into action.

The gun's barrel slid away from his neck as he spun left. He grasped the barrel and drove his right fist straight into the man's Adams' apple. The man clutched his throat, releasing his rifle and gagged for breath. Jake kicked him in the knee and the kidnapper collapsed on the roadway.

Jake spun the weapon around into a firing position and glanced up at the blue bus's windows. The other two kidnappers had their backs turned to him as they worked down the aisle of seats. The two men by the truck were absorbed in talking. Jake kicked the fallen man in the head, stooped over and jerked his gun belt off. He slid it across his own chest and grabbed the man's sheath knife, jamming it into his leather belt in the small of his back.

One of the smokers, noticing his fallen companion, yelped for his friend to look, "Mira! Mira!" He pointed to Jake and raised his weapon.

Jake fired. The man spun around and catapulted head first into the truck's side. Jake didn't wait. He bolted for the woods, zigzagging to dodge bullets that sliced through the air around him. Feet flying, he scrambled down the slope to a wide, fast flowing river, grabbing saplings, sliding and stumbling. Fear-induced adrenaline surged through him and kept him on his feet. Glancing back, he saw the bus pull away. All the kidnappers sprinted after him.

I hope they're all safe and they're going for help. Especially the girl and baby.

At the water's edge, he turned downriver and sprinted along the shore. He leaped over low brush and scooted around trees, his ground-eating stride gobbling up the river's stony shoreline. As he hurdled a fallen tree, his toe hit a branch and he crashed onto his chest, arms outstretched to protect his rifle. He pushed up and sprinted. Three hand made wooden canoes bobbed in the water, prows pulled onto the shore. Jake shoved two boats adrift and piled into the third. He dropped the rifle in the bottom beside two paddles. Grabbing one, he plunged it deep into the swift moving water.

I hope that guy I shot isn't dead. He looked like a rag doll after hitting the truck, though.

A rifle cracked from the trees and the blast gave him added strength. He drove the paddle into the river and the boat hurled downstream.

Another rifle shot rang out and he felt the slight movement of air as the bullet whirred past his head. The dugout neared a curve in the river. Jake cut right, as close to the shoreline as possible.

A bullet thudded into a tree on the riverbank, not more than two feet away. He powered the boat around the curve, safe for a moment and slowed, gasping. He couldn't maintain such an insane pace for long.

I wish I'd had time to sink those other boats.

Jake had canoed many times, but this dugout was heavier and rode lower in the water than the aluminum versions he was used to. He thrust the paddle deep and came within an inch of capsizing. In no time, he got the hang of it. While his heart slowed its jackhammer pounding, he settled into a steady rhythm.

Now Jake took time to look at the river and the jungle surrounding it. Early that morning, his trip had begun in Mexico's Yucatan Peninsula headed for the state of Chiapas. Jake had planned to meet his father in the city of Oaxaca, another eight-hour bus ride. His dad, a magazine publisher, often worked in Mexico where one of his monthlies was based.

In the distance, a monkey's piercing cry cut across the water, drawing him back to the present.

Where's this river taking me? I need a new plan.

Once around the bend, the narrow waterway widened to the width of a football field. He paddled downriver through the still water and the silent, red mangrove forest. To someone who had grown up around evergreen forests, the mangroves created an other-worldly atmosphere, their massive root systems thrusting up high above the river into their trunks. In the thick jungle growth, saw grass clustered around the tree roots, along with sword ferns and strangler vines. Jake hoped he wouldn't have to travel through that mess. Not without a machete, anyway. He studied his newly acquired M14 service rifle. It contained a 20-round magazine, had a web sling, a 22-inch barrel and a walnut stock. Old, but well kept. He remembered about military weapons from his Marine Corps uncle.

Far off, a frightening roar brought images of big cats and feeding frenzies. Goosebumps popped up all over his arms and down his back. The howler monkey screamed again. As he paddled deeper into the jungle, birds sang in the forest's canopy. They were not familiar bird sounds. Some sounded like painful human wailing. He shivered, reminded of the horror of his escape.

Jake had never seen a man shot before, let alone shot one himself. He'd reacted instinctively, just trying to survive, yet now it all seemed like a bad dream. Had he actually shot someone? His stomach turned as the image of the man plunging head first into the truck replayed in his mind. He shuddered as the bile rose, gulping it down. He stopped paddling and bent over at the waist for a few moments.

Jake sat up, took several deep breaths and paddled hard. The wooded banks slipped past as he looked for a place to beach the canoe. He needed time to rest, but a solid wall of mangroves barred his way. He coasted close to shore. A few feet away, the reeds wavered, catching his eyes. A bulging, unblinking amber eye peered through the thick underbrush. Moments later, a twelve-foot crocodile slid across the muddy riverbank and plopped into the water. Within seconds, the croc submerged without a trace. Breathing fast, Jake searched for others waiting in the swamp grass. He shifted course toward the river's center.

Mud tugged at the hull and the boat clung to the silt. Tired now, Jake slipped his shoes and socks off and swung his bare feet into the water. He inhaled sharply as the stupidity of what he'd done hit him. His legs were bait for whatever might lie in wait in the river; the crocodile, water snakes, maybe piranhas. Not knowing what lurked in the tall grass and muck made it worse. His body trembled as if he'd gotten a chill.

Jake seized the boat and dragged it off the mud bank. While he towed it to a tiny beach, a shout from upriver stopped him. Two canoes rounded the last bend in the river.

Oh, no. I knew I should have sunk them. Now what do I do?

Two kidnappers paddled each dugout. If that wasn't enough, something slimy slithered over his bare feet.

Uh, oh. What next? I need to get to land.

Jake's stomach churned and he shuffled his feet to scare away anything nearby. He hoped. He knew he was better off not thinking about it. But it was impossible not to. He remembered the big croc.

2

Jake beached the canoe with a mighty heave, jerking his feet from danger.

Phew. I made it and I still have both feet.

Dropping to his knees on the pebbled beach, he yanked the M14 from the dugout. He squinted, shielding his eyes from the harsh sunlight. A rifle shot cracked. A canoe streaked toward him. He flung himself behind his dugout, poked his head over the bow, caught a glimpse and ducked. Moving to the other end of the boat, he peered over the stern, aimed his rifle and fired. A bullet thunked into the boat.

Close! Oh, no. I left my boots and socks in the canoe. I won't get far without 'em.

He gritted his teeth, popped up and grabbed his footwear. Jake dove back to the beach as a kidnapper's bullet slammed into his canoe, rolled to his side and slipped them on. He would have to run for it.

How do I get out of this mess. No one knows I'm here. No one's looking for me.

The bandits closed in and held their positions in the river's center. Jake fired, this time over the bow. He missed his target, the bullet hitting the hull of the approaching dugout.

I've got to take more time and make every bullet count. Last winter, I had no trouble bagging that deer. But it wasn't shooting back.

From behind a cedar tree came a soft husky voice. "You! Come." Startled, he twisted and looked over his shoulder. In the mangroves' shadows, a dark form beckoned. "Hurry."

Jake swung around with his rifle and scooted into the dense brush on his hands and knees.

I don't think they saw me. I hope not. Hope filled him. *Maybe I will get out of this mess.*

He stood behind the thick tree trunk in time to see someone vanish down the faint trail, moving in silence, like a human hovercraft. Jake followed, breaking branches and stepping on dead wood. The kidnappers' dim voices echoed across the water and into the thick jungle. As he plunged deeper into the moss-bearded trees, they faded away.

I can't see the path anymore. Where is he? Jake stopped, spun in a circle, but his eyes couldn't penetrate the vegetation. *Am I lost already?*

A dark form emerged from giant ferns. After the phantom stepped forward, she halted ten feet in front of him.

Wow. That's definitely not a he.

There was no hesitancy about her. She looked him up and down, but he couldn't tell if she approved or disapproved. Older than Jake, but still a teenager, she stood about five feet eight inches. She had smooth muscles and cheekbones so high and sharp he feared they might puncture her skin. Interwoven black hair hung down her back close to her scalp in a single braid, an arrangement that emphasized her smoky gray eyes.

Except for those eyes, I'd think she was an Indian. Maybe half.

Below a narrow, straight nose, a sensuous mouth widened into a bewitching smile. Her eyes sparkled and everything about her softened.

"Come. We have to be gone when they get to shore." Her song-like voice was intoxicating. Pivoting, she led the way into the lush, green rain forest. Her long, slender legs rippled with muscles. Giving no feeling of haste, each motion flowed into the next. Her machete was out of its sheath and grasped in her hand, her bow and arrows slung across her back, she moved so fast he huffed and puffed to keep up. He'd never met a girl like her before. Only when she paused to hack away the thick undergrowth did Jake, chest heaving, have a chance to catch his breath. She melted through brush he had to push aside and she made no noise.

"Not much farther and we'll take a rest," she said, glancing at Jake.

Jake's body, soaked in sweat, trembled. The oppressive heat and humidity plus lack of water and food were doing him in. It seemed they had been slogging through the jungle for hours. The sight of his tireless new friend slipping through the trees ahead of him kept him going. She moved with the swiftness and ease of a jungle animal. Also the wariness.

Come on, Jake. Find that something extra. Look at her go.

He had psyched himself up to keep going when they stepped from the thick foliage into a clearing facing a waterfall and emerald lagoon. Water cascaded over a rocky cliff jutting up fifty feet. The falls thundered down, throwing a fine mist over their faces. Jungle vegetation spread out on both sides of the falls and surrounded the clearing. The cool and inviting green pool appeared to be deep enough to swim in.

Sunlight streaked through the green canopy's opening made by the pool, but the rest of the perimeter was dark from the denseness of the jungle cover and undergrowth.

"We'll cool off, now." She dropped her weapons in the tall grass, stripped off her Levi shorts, denim halter-top and a pair of dark running shoes and waded out to the falls, clothes in hand. She rinsed them out and tossed them on the grassy bank. Jake's heart skipped a couple of beats at the sight of her flawless, fine-grained brown skin. Her midriff showed the kind of abs he'd always wished he had. She had small hips and firm breasts.

He followed and peeled off his clothes down to his shorts, rinsing them and tossing them near hers and his rifle. Wading out, he plunged beneath the cool water and surfaced, energized. The escape from the bandits and the trek through the jungle had left him drained.

"The water's pure. You can drink it," she said.

He drank too much, holding his mouth open under the falls. His belly bloated. It was not a new experience. He'd done the same thing after dehydrating to make weight to wrestle and being unable to control his thirst anymore.

"Let's go behind the falls. It's cool and hidden there." She waded through the deep pool and led him behind the veil of plummeting water and mist. They sat side by side on a natural stone bench. Jake caught an occasional glimpse of the outside through the thick wall of water.

This is fantastic. Feels 100 degrees cooler here. He looked at his incredible companion.

"Who are you?" Jake blushed at the bluntness of his question and added, "I'm Jake."

"Chanti. Short for Chantico. My dad named me after the Aztec goddess of fires and volcanoes."

"Thanks for your help. I don't know how I would have gotten out of that mess."

"No problem. I watched. You should take more time aiming. Too big a hurry. You'll get better. Why're they after you?"

"They tried to kidnap me from a bus. I shot one of them while escaping. I'm on my way to Oaxaca to see my dad. I stayed in Cancun for a week visiting a local Mexican family my dad knows. They have a son my age, Rafael, who showed me a lot of Mayan ruins like Tulum and Cobá." The words spilled out.

What's the matter with me? Why am I so nervous?

"Why you?" Chanti asked.

"Dad's wealthy. Maybe they knew his name. Maybe they were looking for me. What're you doing in the jungle? You seem to know it like you've always lived here."

"I have. My dad came from the U.S. and my mom was Lacandon Indian, pureblooded Maya descendants. I grew up speaking English to Dad and Maya to Mom. I learned Spanish, too."

"Haven't you ever lived in the U.S.?"

"No. Dad never went back to the States. He loved the jungle's challenge and the simplicity of life here. Two years ago, he and Mom died in a river accident. Most of the time since then, I've been living by myself."

"How old're you?"

"Seventeen. You?"

"Fifteen."

"You look older."

Jake blushed. He had a hard time keeping his gaze on her face.

Chanti looked into his eyes while a mischievous sparkle gleamed in hers.

"Let's get dressed." They both rose.

He stood about five inches taller, broad shouldered and small waisted. Jake had short, sandy hair and dark eyes, the opposite of Chanti.

She admired his lean and well muscled form. "You look like you can handle yourself, not like some of the fat gringos I've seen. One thing you must remember . . . the jungle's unforgiving. One mistake and you're dead. Consider everyone and everything an enemy until he's proven to be a friend. Now, let's go. Those bandits could track us." Chanti led the way from behind the falls.

The padding of big feet rustled over the noise of the water. A branch cracked and through the trees a dark form stole by.

3

"Puma. Probably wants a drink," Chanti said.

Wishing he had his M14 in his hands, Jake's eyes followed the shadowy form. "Looks big."

Chanti waded from the chest high water. "The puma's gone."

Jake followed, diverting his eyes from her to the forest's trees. As they dressed, he scanned the lush green jungle.

Is that puma waiting? Stalking us?

He pivoted and looked at the jungle-enclosed pool and waterfall. He couldn't spot the trail they had arrived on. Without his new companion, he was lost.

"Why weren't your dad and mom with you?" Chanti buttoned her shorts.

"They're divorced. I haven't seen my dad for a year. He's rich and works in Mexico part of the year."

"What's he do?"

"Publishes a monthly magazine here. He likes the Mexican people and probably wouldn't believe someone'd kidnap me. Since he was going to be in Mexico, he gave me a vacation in Cancun. I was on my way to meet him in Oaxaca."

"Where's your mom?"

"She's still at our ranch in New Mexico."

Dressed now, Chanti motioned for Jake to follow. She vanished into the jungle through a veil of vegetation. As Jake stepped under a mango tree, a branch snapped overhead. He glanced up. Four feet above, a six-foot iguana crawled toward him like a prehistoric monster.

It hissed and Jake gasped. He ducked, shrunk away from it and raised the M14. The big lizard's rough skin gleamed bright green with black stripes on its tail. Pointy scales protruded along its back. Long fingers and claws made up the rest of its arsenal.

"Don't worry. Iguanas aren't dangerous. They're good climbers and are usually up about forty or fifty feet above the ground," Chanti said, a sparkle in her eyes.

"They're sure ugly, though. Do they bite?"

"Normally not. They're usually vegetarians, but will eat meat. Some people kill them for food, but not me. They call them bamboo chicken."

"I didn't know they got that big. The ones I've seen must be babies." Jake shivered and looked in the direction they had been headed. "Where're we going?"

"My camp isn't far. It'll be dark soon and we'll stay there. One thing you need to watch for is snakes. Many are poisonous and the boa constrictors are sometimes aggressive. A big one can do a lot of damage."

Jake stayed close behind Chanti. Impenetrable vegetation surrounded them. The shadows appeared to move. The sun sank low and he didn't want to lose her.

How does she move like that? She makes practically no sound. I feel clumsy and I've spent a lot of time in the woods.

But something about being close to Chanti comforted Jake; he felt safe.

They trudged about a mile through the jungle. Chanti's shorts and halter-top were soaked with sweat.

She's not so different from me.

It was dense with cedar and enormous chicle trees, twelve feet in diameter and two hundred feet high. Roots, often three feet around, jutted high above the ground, sometimes high enough for Jake to walk under. Strangler vines wrapped around the trunks and traveled upward.

Chanti and Jake climbed high on a mound. She still had a spring in her step. They encountered an army of leaf-cutter ants in single file dragging leaves ten times larger than their bodies. Pausing on top to watch their progress, Chanti spoke, "Wouldn't it be nice to be that strong?" She looked toward the nearby hillside. "This mound we're on is probably a dirt-covered temple or some other type of Maya ruin. They're everywhere. The jungle grows over everything." She headed in the same direction they'd been traveling. "It's not far now."

Creepers lashed themselves to tree trunks and heliconias hung, looking like multi-colored lobster claws. Along a narrow path, philodendrons climbed into the shadows of chicle trees. Overhead, lianas draped from the immense canopy, the vines binding the forest's cover into a single interwoven net blocking the sun blazing overhead. The forest floor held an eerie quiet.

Sweat soaked every inch of Jake's clothes. His chest heaved and he stumbled. Rotting vegetation six inches deep gave off a peculiar, but not unpleasant odor. It reminded Jake of being inside a green house on a hot day. As he wondered if they'd ever get there, the trees thinned and gave way to a sunlit clearing, dominated by a native hut with thick roofing of sun bleached and rain toughened palm fronds. It backed up to a small stream. The walls, made of sticks, enclosed all four sides except for the small doorway opening, which let in light and air.

Following Chanti inside, Jake stepped up on trembling legs and ducked to enter.

Wow. I can hardly stand. If I don't get a drink soon, I'll pass out. Come on, Jake. Buck up.

"Welcome. It's not much by your standards, but it's one of the places I stay. It keeps the rain off."

Jake said, "Nice hammock." He grinned, determined not to show his fatigue, as he added, "No TV?"

She smiled back. "But I have another hammock for you stored above mine."

He stood on the hut's rough plank flooring raised a foot off the ground. Beyond a crude wooden table and two rickety chairs in the room's center, a woven hammock hung from a crosspiece. Draped netting kept out the mosquitoes and bugs. Old cooking and eating utensils lay scattered on the table.

Jake glanced up. Besides the extra hammock, a substantial arrow supply and two more bows hung suspended on ropes fastened to the same crosspiece. "You're prepared for a war. Where're your other places?"

"I've another in the jungle a few kilometers from here and one in my grandma's village."

"I'm dying for water." Jake eyed the nearby stream. "Is that safe to drink?" He pointed through the door to the babbling water.

"Sure. It's spring fed. Follow me. We still haven't come across any snakes yet, but always be on the lookout. Even the local Lacondans get bitten by them. I know several who have died from snakebites and I don't want that to happen to you. Always empty your shoes before you put them on. They're a favorite place for scorpions, spiders and snakes."

Jake listened to her advice seriously. He had already seen plenty of danger and realized without her he had no chance.

She showed him where to drink. "Before you kneel down, be positive there's nothing to harm you. The jungle shows no mercy. It only recognizes strength. The strong rule. When you drink from the river, you have to watch for crocodiles and cayman as well as snakes."

"Are there piranhas in the river?"

"No. They're only in South America."

Chanti handed Jake one of two clay mugs. Jake dipped his homemade mug into the stream. He downed the first cup in one gulp.

"Hey! Slow down. You'll get sick."

They sipped their fill and headed back to the hut. Dusk neared and everything changed. The air cooled. The light turned to amber and the open sky above filled with darting swallows. Jake heard the sharp cries of hundreds of other birds wheeling through the darkening sky. Hawks, herons, colorful cackling parrots, toucans and scarlet macaws flitted through the trees, landing and flying off again. Two spider monkeys played in a tree on the clearing's edge.

Chanti said, "This time of day is great. It's cooler and birds're everywhere. Come. There's not much to eat, but I have some jerky and avocados. We'll kill some meat tomorrow." Jake liked the way she included him. "First, let's get the other hammock down."

The hut darkened so Chanti lit a big tan candle fixed in its own wax to the tabletop. By the time they had the second hammock and its netting hung, Jake's stomach wouldn't stop growling. The jerky and avocados tasted like fine cuisine.

It had grown pitch dark. Rain patted the roof, then drummed. In no time it became a torrential downpour, so loud Jake thought the roof would cave in. An hour later, it stopped. The air turned cooler. Jake heard a strange drone everywhere. "What's the hum I hear?"

"Insects. Make sure your net is secure. They rule after dark. Silence returns at dawn. The air's still and mist rises from the cool ground. It's one of my favorite times."

"Right now I'm too tired to appreciate it."

"You've had a tough day and need some sleep. I'll wait till you're settled and I'll put the candle out. Remember to knock out your shoes before you put them on in the morning."

"Okay." Jake struggled into his hammock, too tired to talk. He wanted to ask if she could get him to civilization, but that would wait. The hammock tilted to the opposite side. It came close to dumping him. He stabilized it at the last second, as it swung from side to side, creaking. He pulled the netting down around him.

Chanti chuckled as she began sharpening her machete at the table with a whetstone. In a few minutes she finished and blew out the candle. She padded across the floor to her own hammock. "Good night, Jake."

"Night, Chanti."

What a day. Nearly kidnapped, shot someone and saved by a beautiful female Tarzan. How'd I get into this mess?

For a few minutes, visions of the man spinning into the truck haunted him. He tasted bile again.

I wonder how those kidnappers knew I was on the bus.

Moments later, Jake fell into a deep sleep, exhausted by the day's adventures.

When he awoke in the early dawn, a brawny shadow lurked in the doorway.

The shape chilled his blood.

4

An enormous cat lay silhouetted in the dark doorway, stretched out, head up, watching. Jake's heart pounded. He was scared, but not paralyzed. He held his breath as his sweaty palms searched for the rifle.

The hammock's confined limits didn't give him enough room to use his weapons. *I'm practically helpless. Swell, my rifle's on the floor. Only my knife.*

The shadow rose from the floor. Huge, dark. Jake's heart beat faster, pounding against his chest. The soft thud of the big cat's padding feet headed for Chanti's hammock amid subdued growling.

As he opened his mouth to shout to Chanti.

"Ba lam, my baby. Where've you been? It's okay, Jake. This is Ba lam. He's been my friend since he was a baby. Just don't move too fast at first."

A dim ray of early dawn light illuminated the doorway. The growling changed to purring and grew louder. As Jake slipped from his hammock, almost dumping himself on the floor, the fierce, unblinking yellow eyes turned in his direction. Jake's legs still trembled. Chanti stood by her hammock. Ba lam purred louder and rubbed his head so hard against Chanti, he staggered her. The beast flopped down and rolled over. Chanti dove onto him, rough housing and wrestling.

She's crazy. That cat could rip her apart.

She rubbed his belly and bounced to her feet again, "Come, Jake. Meet Ba lam. Ba lam is Maya for jaguar." Chanti rubbed and caressed the big cat's head. "Ba lam's a black jaguar, only two years old

so he's not full grown, yet. Ba Lam, this is Jake."
She put her hand on Jake's shoulder.

Jake edged his hand out for the jaguar to
sniff. Light streamed in the open doorway now and
Ba lam's burning yellow eyes and huge white teeth
glowed against his black face. A low rumbling
growl greeted his hand. Jake eased it back so as not
to startle the cat.

"Don't worry. He'll get used to you. He's
never been around another human."

"He's big. His head's huge and his front legs
and shoulders are, too. He looks like a leopard on
steroids. How much bigger'll he get?"

"Maybe another 50 to 100 pounds. He must
be close to 250, now. When we're outside in the
sunlight, you'll be able to see his faint spots through
the black. They're the same as a regular jaguar has,
but very faint."

"Are there many others around here?"

"No. Jaguars here are rare now. Man's been
cutting and burning forests, disrupting their normal
hunting and traveling patterns. This jungle might
not be here much longer. It's getting smaller and
smaller."

"I remember in a movie seeing a jaguar
swimming in a river."

"Yeh. They catch fish, too, and often tackle
turtles and large cayman."

"When Mom and I were in Costa Rica last
summer, I remember seeing what one did to a huge
sea turtle. Just the shell was left."

"They're also good climbers. They hunt
monkeys in the lower branches of large trees. If you
hear a strange sound like a loud, raspy cough, it's

probably a jaguar. They don't roar, but snarl and cough and growl."

"What else does he eat?"

"Peccaries or wild pigs, deer, sloths, tapirs and smaller animals. Look at Ba lam now. He acts hungry. Let's get started." She rubbed Ba lam's head.

"We'll see if we can shoot a peccary or tapir. Our best bet is near the river. Yesterday, we went inland from the river to the waterfall and then angled back toward the river again. We're downriver from where you landed." Chanti turned back to the table.

"I almost forgot," she said, handing him a viscous red substance in a pan. "Rub this into your skin. It'll make it red, but it repels insects. It's from the achiote plant."

As Jake rubbed it on his arms, legs and face, he thought it looked like war paint. Chanti joined him, spreading it on herself. They smiled at each other when surveying the finished job.

Wow. In the jungle she's stoic, but when she smiles at me it turns my legs to rubber.

"Before we go, I have to whiz," Jake said, a blush spreading up through his face.

"Peeing isn't a problem. Just don't do it near the stream. Solid waste can be a difficulty. We don't want to leave it near our camp. Find a big rock like this." She reached down to place her hand on one. "Turn it over and dig out the dirt underneath and when you're done, fill in the dirt and set the rock back on top. Then wash yourself. You can use leaves first if you want, but afterward wash yourself. Get rid of solid waste everyday. Wash everyday. You don't want any disease or infection. Rinse your clothes out whenever you can. Be very careful there's nothing to harm you close by; no snakes or scorpions or wild boars."

Jake jogged into the jungle downstream and returned a few minutes later.

"Thanks. You make things easier." He didn't know any girls back in New Mexico who would have given him that explanation, even if they could.

They gathered their hunting gear and she led the way. Chanti's sharp eyes saw what Jake hadn't, an indiscernible opening in the dense growth. They plunged into the jungle through the early morning mist, following a faint trail. Jake realized, with the jaguar's appearance, he had forgotten to ask Chanti about getting him back to civilization.

Chanti's something else. I don't think I want to go back right now. Besides, I'll never have an adventure like this again. Maybe I can at least let Mom know I'm safe, though.

Ba lam forced his way to the front. Jake saw little of the mysterious black cat as it stalked ahead of Chanti through the thick growth. Twice the jaguar coughed hoarsely.

Chanti stopped in front of him as the savage jaguar snarled. She moved aside to allow Jake to see. Wading through a marshy pool in the moist forest, Ba lam had leaped onto a tapir taking a morning drink. Blackish-brown with whitish face, throat and chest, the tapir bucked and squeaked. Its short legged, heavy body put up a struggle, but the powerful cat bit right through the skull bones, causing instant death. Clambering through the trees above, howler monkeys roused the jungle with their intimidating roars. Ba lam dragged the large beast into the jungle.

"Sometimes we share, but he doesn't seem to want to this time. Maybe because you're here. Tapirs are strange looking animals with their long, fleshy flexible snout. There's nothing else like 'em. They can weigh up to 600 pounds and have four toes on their front feet and three on the rear. That one is probably three hundred pounds." Chanti led again. "We'll find something ahead."

"Here, lend me your machete and let me lead."

"Wait a while. The path widens ahead and you'll see more. Right now you might not see something important, okay?"

Jake realized the statement's truth, and it didn't faze him. *I'd be lost or dead by now without her.*

It warmed up and Jake wiped sweat from his brow.

I won't have any trouble making my wrestling weight next season at this rate. If I ever get out of here.

Chanti made her way with ease through the tangled brush, avoiding the vines that trailed from the tree branches and the roots that reached up to trip her. They trekked through a confined gorge, clogged with brush. At last, reaching its far end, they inched across a narrow ledge above a large pool of water. One misstep and they would plunge into the lagoon.

A log floated two feet from the ledge. Poking from the scaly log's top, stared two bulging, amber eyes, riveted on him. On closer inspection, another floated two feet to its side.

Crocodiles. I see now why she said 'one mistake and you're dead.' But what I see with fright, she accepts as an everyday happening. I've never known anyone so young who's so capable and cool.

Once they crossed in safety, the trail widened.

"If you still want to lead, go to it. We're not too far from the river now."

"Thanks. I know I have a lot to learn, but I'll try to do it fast." Jake set out along the trail, trying to watch everywhere at once. After a short time, a two-foot long tri-colored snake wriggled along the path toward him.

Whoa. That's a coral snake. I've seen them in the States.

Jake grabbed a heavy branch from the trail's side and squashed its head. Using the branch, he flipped the snake off the path and into the trees.

"Good," said Chanti. "You're catching on. Never hesitate. If you do, you'll be dead."

Smiling, head up and chest out, Jake kept moving at a fast pace. Attracted to her, he worried the two years difference in their ages would make her think less of him. He remembered when he'd tried to ask Shari Lane out. A senior, she'd listened patiently while he stuttered his way through the invitation, but turned him down.

The river gushing around boulders thundered through the jungle's growth.

"Slow down. There might be animals drinking from the river. Be ready."

Jake returned the machete to Chanti and readied his rifle to fire. Chanti's presence calmed rather than disturbed him.

Her competence is affecting me. Her even temperament doesn't put any pressure on me. She lets me be myself.

He promised himself he wouldn't miss. A faint breeze brought a strange gamy smell. He edged his way onto the river's bank. Fifty yards down, two peccaries, front legs immersed, drank river water. Jake had seen them in Arizona. Javelina, the Spaniards had called them. Pig like, hoofed mammals having dense, long, dark-gray bristles and a collar of white hair. Much smaller than the tapir.

Hey, not so hard to carry.

He could kill them both, but decided to only take one. No refrigeration for the second. He raised his rifle and fired. The nearest animal gave a convulsive leap straight up and flopped down on the stone covered two-foot wide beach. The other wheeled and disappeared into the jungle.

"Good shot. I'm glad you didn't shoot the second. Let's make sure its dead, although it looked like a heart shot to me." She set off down the shoreline and Jake followed. "It probably weighs about 50 or 60 pounds. We'll butcher it at camp." They gutted the wild pig and Jake slung it over his shoulder. He had learned to butcher meat while hunting in New Mexico, as well as working on their cattle ranch.

As they trekked back to the trail, Chanti sniffed and paused.

"Kidnapper," Jake's hoarse voice whispered. A short, gaunt man in camouflage fatigues had stepped out from around a large tree and blocked their way. The man grinned at them with great gaps in his stained teeth. He showed no respect for Chanti's prowess and Jake's hands were full. Stained Teeth held his rifle in relaxed hands pointed between them.

Chanti's hand flew to her machete, whipped it out and threw it in a blur. The gleaming, long razor-edged machete streaked through the air. It buried itself in the man's throat. Blood spurted and he toppled over backward clutching it. A few convulsive struggles and he died, smile wiped from his face.

It happened so fast, Jake stood dumbfounded, unable to move. Now he dropped the peccary and lifted his M 14, ready to use.

"He must have heard the shot. He couldn't believe a female and a young man could cause him harm. Pick up the meat, but keep your rifle ready." She sprinted to the fallen kidnapper and jerked her machete from his throat. She wiped the blood on his filthy shirt and jogged back.

For the first time, Jake checked out the big knife. She had sharpened both sides of the blade. It looked like he could shave with it.

"Look at my hand." Chanti held it up. Her hand trembled. "I've never killed anyone before." She stared at it and dropped it to her side. "Let's go."

Leading the way, Chanti set off to retrace their route from the river. Behind them a branch snapped.

Chanti's head spun toward the sound.

When the shot rang out, the impact wobbled Jake.

5

The bullet struck the dead peccary. It spun Jake around, slamming him into Chanti's back. Staggered, she kept her footing. Jake righted himself, looking back at the husky kidnapper.

"Off the trail," Jake blurted out in a hoarse voice.

He dove to the right, spilling the dead pig ahead of him. The man aimed again. Chanti had already plunged to the other side. The bandit fired.

Too late. Jake returned the fire. His target had ducked out of sight.

Make every shot count.

Chanti had disappeared. Jake scanned the surrounding jungle. *Can't worry, now. I'd better take care of myself. Maybe she's circling back.* He peered through the brush, but nothing moved.

He waited, not an easy thing for a fifteen-year-old to do. Sweat dripped into his eyes. Branches broke deeper in the jungle.

She doesn't make noise. It must be the kidnappers. I can't stay here. Why do they want me so bad?

Jake threaded his way toward the place he'd last seen the burly kidnapper chief. He crept along, moving objects from his path that would make noise. All the while, his gaze scanned the forest.

"Jake," Chanti shouted. Gritting his teeth and tensing all his muscles against a bullet's impact, he rose and sprinted across the trail toward her voice. He slowed as soon as he hit the dense greenery. A short distance into the woodland, he spotted a small clearing through a break in the foliage.

Five men armed with rifles stood in a circle facing the clearing's perimeter. In the center, a sixth gripped Chanti's hair from behind, yanking her head back and laying his knife at her taut throat. Blood dripped to her collarbone, but her expression showed nothing.

Look how brave she is. She's amazing. I have to save her.

Jake leaned against a tree trunk, his heart pounding, rifle pointed at the enemy. The kidnapper's short, powerful leader stood to Chanti's left. There was enough space between branches for Jake to have a clear view of the knifeman. He didn't recognize the filthy, ugly man with yellow teeth. None of the six had seen him yet.

Don't hesitate. Chanti's life's at stake.

Jake aimed with care. He drew and expelled several deep breaths to quiet his nerves.

In all the movies depicting a similar situation he'd seen, the man with the gun always gave up his advantage. He hated that. If they were good shots, how could they miss. A man with a bullet in his brain isn't going to cut someone's throat. He took in a breath and eased out half. As he sighted on the left eye of the man with the knife at Chanti's throat, he gently squeezed the trigger. The rifle fired. Its bullet rocketed into the man's eye where Jake had aimed. Blood and gore sprayed out the back of his head. The knife hand fell away as the man crumpled. Chanti vanished.

Relieved, but marveling at how fast she reacted, Jake shifted his aim. Only one bandit remained standing as the others dove and flattened out or ducked behind tree trunks. The tree's branches prevented him from having a clean shot. He ducked down and darted back the way he'd come as a bullet plowed into a tree three feet away. As much as he wanted to run full out, he imitated Chanti's silent passage through the jungle. Branches cracked as one stupid man charged after him. He wheeled and fired at the noise. He didn't think he hit anything, but the noise stopped. They would think twice, now.

When he reached the trail again, he sprinted to the spot he had dropped the pig. Already ants covered its carcass. He dropped to his knees, brushed off a multitude of insects, lifted the pig and slung it over his shoulder. Still on his knees, Jake looked back. Nothing moved. Only jarring monkey screeches filled the air. He struggled a little with the weight, rose and jogged down the narrow trail until he rounded a curve.

Slowing, he glanced down at his clothes, soaking wet from sweat. His hands shook.

What now? Come on, think.

He gagged as he saw the man's head explode again, but when he remembered the man's knife drawing blood from Chanti's throat, he didn't feel so bad.

He continued along the path, wondering, but not for long.

He had been looking at the rocky trail so he wouldn't trip. When he looked up, she stood in front of him. Blood had dried on her throat from the shallow cut.

With a trembling hand, she wiped sweat from her brow. "I didn't know if I should call you or not. I was scared and I couldn't think of any other way. Thanks for not hesitating. That wasn't an easy shot to make with so much at stake." She gave a strained smile and, leaning into him, kissed his cheek. "Thank you, Jake."

Jake's chest puffed and he blushed. *I wish I didn't do that. Grow up, Jake.* "We'd better move. They won't stay put for long."

Chanti turned to lead the way. She had retrieved her weapons. His legs trembled a little, threatened to give out, but he wouldn't let Chanti know. He was getting used to eating once a day, but he didn't like it. His shoulder and neck ached and grew stiff from the peccary. His back ached. Everything ached.

I can do this. I've got something more in the tank. This pig's as light as a feather. He grinned to himself. The peccary weighed less.

"We're going back a different way. I know a spring where we can get water and cook some meat. Okay with you?"

"Sounds good if you think it's safe." At this point, Jake wasn't sure he cared. They hiked on, no longer on the trail. The going grew much rougher. Denser. Expecting another long trek, Jake's mouth dropped open when they struggled from the tangled foliage into a tiny clearing with a small spring-fed pool. Relieved, he threw the pig onto a carpet of leaves and they both lay down to gulp water from the clear lagoon.

Chanti dug a fire pit, scraping the soft ground with a dead branch. Jake collected dry wood. Chanti plucked a match from a waterproof container carried in her pant's pocket and lit a near smokeless fire. The small amount of smoke drifted through the branches, dissipating in the thick forest canopy. Jake cut two chunks of meat and with sharpened sticks, roasted them. The mouth-watering smell of the sizzling meat made Jake's stomach rumble. They ate in silence and Jake sliced another piece when he finished. He held it up to Chanti, but she shook her head. When he had wolfed down the last morsel, they drank again from the spring.

"I'm sorry I put you in such a spot. I underestimated them, both in number and brains. After telling you to be so careful, I wasn't. I'm ashamed," Chanti said, chin up, looking into Jake's eyes. "I haven't run into trouble like that before. You saved my life. I won't forget."

Jake's eyes grew large. She was so frank. He valued honesty. She had none of the frivolous manners of girls he knew at home. "How do you stay so calm? You didn't look like you were afraid when he had the knife at your throat. I was scared hiding behind the trees."

"It's all attitude. If you get up in the morning and think you'll feel bad, you will. But, if you decide you're going to feel good, you will. If you accept you're afraid, you'll always be afraid. I choose not to live in fear. There's death everywhere in the jungle. I'd be afraid all day, every day. Instead, I welcome the challenge. Risks make life exciting and way more fun. It's probably easier for me because I don't have anyone close to worry about. My dad loved that about the jungle and it's why he chose to live here instead of back in the States. He was doing what he loved, challenging the river, when he and Mom died. They got caught in rapids, overturned and thrown into some rocks. I wouldn't be surprised if they were both grinning when it happened. I was sad at first, but I remember thousands of good things and I feel warm inside." There was a softness about Chanti, now. She was not just granite. A few tears trickled down her cheeks. "I don't mean I'm never afraid, I was back there. But I've learned how to wipe it from my mind."

"My mom got to be almost as big a risk taker as Dad. She went everywhere with him. They were inseparable and she was always smiling, like she knew something the rest of us didn't. Neither one of them seemed to be afraid and I made up my mind I wouldn't be either. They were some pair. My dad was your size and white and Mom was pure indio and tiny. I loved life with them. When things get tough, I think of them and I feel better. You remind me a lot of my dad."

Jake's heart swelled with pride. He recognized the attitude she talked about was the same he tried to have when he was tired or afraid, only she took it to a higher level. *She can be so fearless, partly because she's so competent and feels in control of her life. But she's not afraid of wild things because she's wild herself.*

"I wish my mom and dad had been that close," Jake said. "I've only seen Dad about once a year since I was ten. This was supposed to be our annual get-together. He's a good guy, but I don't know him very well. You'd like my mom. I hope you can get to know her."

Before they could say more, Chanti raised her hand to silence him. He wasn't sure what she'd heard, but he heard it, too. A disturbance that didn't fit the forest's usual sounds perked up Jake's ears. A murmur that grew louder, then became voices. They were close, because the jungle's density prevented sound from carrying far. Chanti had her bow in hand, arrow ready. Jake lifted his rifle and eased off the safety. The fire was almost out and he nudged some loose dirt over it to finish the job.

6

Jake jerked the peccary up onto his shoulder and melted into the jungle behind Chanti. They paused and listened.

Pop.

His foot squashed a dried out nutshell betraying their location.

The murmur stopped.

The rasping of Jake's breath broke the midday quiet.

Five feet to his left, Chanti drew her bowstring halfway back, her body rigid like Ba lam before springing onto the tapir's back.

Jake knelt, rifle ready, so he'd have a clearer shot.

But there are creatures in the forest far more deadly than man.

As he eased the dead pig to the ground, his eyes came to rest on a discolored clump.

He gulped. Goose bumps prickled his skin.

The clump had a pattern of black-edged triangles, narrow at the top and wide at the bottom, set against olive gray that marked the slender coils of a long snake.

A wedge-shaped head with a yellowish chin and throat sprouted from the ferns. Its vertical eye pupils malevolently stared at Jake. The heat sensing loreal pits looked like extra nostrils. The long black tongue flicked in and out. Chills rushed down his back. He trembled.

The snake's head swayed, but its dead looking eyes never broke contact with Jake.

Paralyzed, Jake couldn't breathe. Before his bus trip, he had seen the serpent in a wild animal park near Cancun. Fer-de-lance, or Barba Amarilla (Yellow Beard) as the Mexicans call them. When it's about to strike, it rears up, with its head and upper body forming an "S" shape. It strikes so fast it's nearly impossible to see it move from that position. It does so with super accuracy even in total darkness. Very aggressive, it hunts mainly at night, but it moves around anytime it wants to.

He knelt face to face with a killer. He waited. From the corner of his eye, he could see Chanti saw it, too. The longest few minutes of his life seemed like an hour. He smiled to himself as he changed his thinking away from fear. *What a story this'll make if I get out alive. The most dangerous snake in the Americas.* It uncoiled to its full length, as long as he was tall. The serpent slithered silently through the grass to a small tree about 15 feet away, stopped and coiled again.

Jake expelled his breath. He had no idea how long he'd held it. Once he took control of his mind, he hadn't been as afraid.

Chanti grasped his shoulder. His thoughts returned to their other problem. Glancing once more back at the Fer-de-lance, he focused on whoever approached their position. They waited in silence. The murmur of voices began again. The thick brush and ferns prevented Jake from seeing anyone. Because of the muffled voices, he didn't recognize the language. He concentrated on a small space he could see through, a narrow tunnel through the vegetation. Something white passed the other end. So intent were both of them on the other side of the green wall, they never saw the man stalking them from the side, his rifle ready.

Chanti and Jake sensed his presence at the same time. A faint sound, perhaps two pant legs brushing together, betrayed the man, only fifteen feet away. They glanced his way. A replica of the other kidnappers, his cruel sneer showed his overconfidence as he looked down his rifle's barrel.

They had no chance.

A long "S" shaped form blurred into motion. It struck the man in the thigh. He shrieked, trying to hit the recoiled viper with his rifle. The snake struck again so fast the man didn't move, this time hitting his hand. He stumbled a few steps and toppled over, crumpling to the ground, throat gurgling. His rifle clattered on a rock. His legs jerked convulsively several times before he stiffened and stopped moving. The Fer-de-lance wriggled away through the ferns.

Jake and Chanti looked at each other, grinning, relief flooding through them.

"Sometimes luck is worth more than skill or knowledge," Chanti leaned close and whispered as she motioned for him to follow and slipped away from the noises into the jungle. "I'm sorry I didn't hear him. I should have. Let's get out of here."

Jake slung the peccary over his left shoulder keeping the M14 in his right hand. The adrenaline kept him pumped up and strong. They wound their way through the tangled roots and ferns. To avoid noise, Chanti didn't use her machete.

Even Chanti breathed hard with the pace she set. When they had gone a ways, her machete flew, chopping away vegetation. *She reminds me of Xena, Warrior Princess, only she uses a machete instead of a sword.* At last she stopped.

"That snake is called Barba Amarilla because of its yellowish chin and throat. It causes more deaths in the Americas than any other reptile. Its bite is fatal for a human. You did the right thing by staying still. I couldn't move without upsetting it, either. You're getting pretty cool under pressure." Her liquid voice sent chills up and down his spine.

"Thanks. I tried to keep the right attitude and it worked. At first, I was scared. Those evil eyes showed no sign of emotion. Then I thought of what you said about fear and I turned it around. It felt good." *I'm surprised I can confess being afraid to a girl. Somehow, it doesn't seem to matter to her, or me.*

Chanti studied Jake. He did remind her of her dad. And he was fast adapting to the jungle's ways. She liked him more and more. Chanti had never had a close friend since she was a child. She grew up too different from the Indian youths. *He has a good heart. We can be friends. I can't let anything happen to him.*

"You're brave, Jake. And a quick learner, too."

A warm glow spread through Jake. This young woman who would fight to the death against any attacker, thought him brave. *I can't let her down.*

She threw a spellbinding smile toward him that caused his legs to wobble. It was blinding, the bright white of her teeth against her face's sun darkened skin. Jake thought of his first sight of Ba lam with the burning golden eyes and huge white teeth glowing against his black face. She and the giant jaguar were alike in many ways.

"Let's get back to my place so we can rest and eat. It's not far now and it'll be dark soon." He followed her into the jungle. She didn't push the pace so hard, but before he knew it, they stepped into the clearing by her hut. *How did she find this place? I didn't see one recognizable landmark.* After the jungle's danger, seeing the flimsy structure filled him with relief. They both strode straight to the stream and gulped their fill of cool water.

"We'll eat and I'll show you how to smoke what's left of the meat," Chanti said. "It'll preserve it for a short time."

They built a fire and cooked two substantial chunks of meat. Jake's mouth watered the whole time. After devouring the semi-cooked peccary, Chanti showed him how to smoke the remainder. They hung the meat in Chanti's specially constructed tiny smoke shack, hidden among the trees on the clearing's edge opposite the stream. Dusk fell across the clearing by the time they finished.

As Jake turned toward their sleeping quarters, he said, "Whoa." His heart thumped and he stopped at the sight of Ba lam lying in the hut's doorway. The big cat had appeared in silence. Even Chanti's mouth dropped open.

"Ba lam! Where've you been?" She trotted to him as he stood, shoulders rippling in the day's last light. She knelt before him, clasping his huge head between her hands. His jumbo pink tongue washed her face as he purred his delight.

She reached back to pull a portion of smoked meat from her bundle. It disappeared into his cavernous mouth. Chanti stood and the immense cat rubbed against her legs as he circled her and reared up on his hind legs and placed his front paws on her shoulders, looking her straight in the eyes. Her knees buckled a little.

"Get off me, you big oaf. You're too big now." She pushed him away and rubbed his head and ears when he returned to all fours.

"Here, Jake. Let's see if he's friendlier this time."

Jake approached Ba lam, extending his hand with another chunk of meat toward those monstrous teeth. It, too, vanished. Ba lam, yellow eyes gleaming against his black face, smelled Jake's hand and rubbed his head against it. Jake scratched his ears and Ba lam purred.

"Great. He likes you. But be a little careful for a while, and don't move too fast around him. Don't startle him. He might react to danger too quickly."

"Gotcha. Even friendly dogs do that sometimes."

Ba lam wandered off. Chanti and Jake stepped up into the hut where she lit a candle. Chanti tied the meat bundle to a cord hanging from a beam and pulled it up, suspending it in the air near the ceiling.

Jake stomped a scorpion near the wall. "I don't know if I can get used to those things or not. Scorpions and big spiders." He kicked it out the open door.

"I'm going to fill this water jug," Chanti said as she headed out the door. Jake stood in the doorway watching as she walked toward the stream. She gasped and froze. "Jake," she breathed.

Straight across the creek, a mountain lion stood immobile on a boulder. Its legs long and heavily muscled, with two enormous, well-padded forepaws. Its unwavering stare scared Jake. The lion had a tawny color with a white underbelly and muzzle. His relatively small head had black tipped, rounded ears and black on its muzzle's sides going from its nose down to its mouth.

Its cold, amber, unblinking eyes glared across at Chanti. He was stalking her.

A terrifying roar and the great tawny body crouched low, rear haunches raised and bunched to spring and launched itself through the air, sailing over the creek toward Chanti.

7

Jake knew he couldn't reach his rifle in time. Still, he darted inside and snatched the M14 from the table.

He sprinted back outside as the big cat landed in front of Chanti, brawny shoulders and hindquarters bulging.

The savage predator catapulted toward her from the stream's bank.

She crouched, machete in hand.

A dark form streaked across the clearing, muscular, powerful.

In midair, Ba lam's leap intersected the puma's with a crashing thump. The collision plunged the puma away from Chanti.

Her upward machete thrust only scratched the puma's chest.

The two biting, tearing, growling beasts rolled over and over, claws and teeth ripping away chunks of flesh. Jake joined Chanti, circling the two fierce carnivores, looking for an opening to help Ba lam. Jake's heart pounded and he gasped for air.

Ba lam needed no help. He sunk his teeth into the nape of the puma's neck and hung on with a grip nothing could break. The same powerful jaws that crushed the tapir's skull, ground deeper into the neck. A minute more and the struggle ended. A tremor ran through the puma's body and it went limp. It had stalked its last victim.

Ba lam rose from the dead cat and, casting a glance over his shoulder, padded a short distance to the stream's bank. He flopped down and rolled onto his back, rubbing it on the ground. Afterwards, he licked his wounds. He bled from a dozen slashes, but acted as though this happened every day.

Chanti ran to him and caressed his immense head. "Ba lam. You saved my life. Nobody's as brave as you."

Jake knelt beside them and said in unsteady tones, "That happened so fast. I'm ashamed. I did nothing." He reached toward Ba lam's head, then hesitated. "He sure is something. It didn't look like anything could stop that puma."

"It happens that way sometimes. So quick. You see why I say not to hesitate? You can lose everything in an instant. I might have survived, but not without some serious injuries. I'm going to put some mud on his wounds."

While she scooped glops of mud from the stream's bank, Jake rubbed Ba lam's head. "Thanks, Ba lam. You were great."

Jake exhaled and drew in several deep breaths. His heart slowed to normal. *Chanti's safe.*

The big jaguar purred deep in his throat. The huge pink tongue slobbered across Jake's face, but rough as it was, he didn't mind a bit. The great feline rubbed his head against Jake's hand and continued licking his wounds.

"It's just another day in the jungle for him," Jake said. "You and he are a lot alike."

Chanti rubbed mud onto Ba lam's wounds. She squinted in the fading light. The jaguar's thick, black coat made it difficult to spot his gashes. "Okay, Big Boy," she said, rubbing his head as she rose. "Let's get inside, Jake. The bugs're getting nasty."

"That red insect repellant you gave me this morning worked all day. Tomorrow I need to talk to you about getting in touch with my mom and dad. They'll be worried. But not now. I'm too tired." Jake climbed into his hammock. "Night, Chanti."

"Good night, Jake. You were fantastic today."

"Thanks."

Numb with fatigue, a momentary pang of guilt for not thinking about his parents knifed through Jake. Sleep refused to come. Thoughts of danger and death plagued his mind. He rolled in his hammock, trying to get comfortable. *I had more adventure and excitement today than I would in a lifetime back home. Met a jaguar, watched him kill a tapir and a puma, then became friends. Met a Fer-de-lance face to face. Watched Chanti save us from a kidnapper and Ba lam save her.* Jake looked down at the M14. *Shot a wild pig and a kidnapper. Nobody back home will ever believe it. Why don't I feel worse about killing somebody? Maybe because they started it and deserved what they got!* He was still numb from the realization. He had killed a man. The scene of the man's head bursting from his shot, made his stomach churn and he gulped. There was emptiness inside him. No sense of right. But the more he thought about those monster kidnappers, the better he felt about what he had done. They'd made their own choice.

Unable to keep his eyes open, Jake slid into darkness while rain lashed the small hut.

At dawn, Jake awoke. A scorpion climbed down the netting of his hammock. He looked twice to see if it crawled on the outside. *Good.* He swatted the inside of the netting, knocking it to the floor. As he swung down, he grabbed a shoe and squashed it.

Chanti watched from her hammock, smiling at him, as he knocked both shoes against the floor to dislodge any creature that might have crawled in during the night. He blushed.

"I was wondering if you'd ever wake up," she said.

"Sorry. I don't mind admitting I was really tired last night."

"Me, too. I don't usually have a day like yesterday."

"I hope not. We crammed a lot into one day. Chanti, I'd like to be able to get in touch with my mom, at least, and maybe my dad. Is there somewhere we can get to a phone?"

"Sometimes there's an Indio in my grandmother's small village who has a satellite phone. That's not too far, but if he's not there we'll have to go to a larger village, which could take some time. It depends on how high the river is. If it's too wild, it'll be hard to cross. Actually, dangerous."

"Don't you have a dugout somewhere?"

"Sure, but here's the problem. The rivers are too long and filled with dangerous rapids. We'd be portaging every few feet in some stretches and my dugout isn't light. The Lacanja River isn't so bad, but the Lacantum and Ucumacinta are wider and treacherous."

"Can't we reach a village going overland?"

"No. The closest village of any size, Piedras Negras, is across the Ucumacinta, but there's no good place to cross close by. We'll head to Grandma Maria's and if the satellite phone's there, no problem."

"That would do it."

"Except we'll still have to arrange to meet your mom somewhere. San Cristobal de las Casas might be the best place, but it's through some pretty awful jungle."

Jake and Chanti knelt in the doorway petting Ba lam's huge head. He hadn't moved since the night before.

"Is he guarding us?" Jake asked.

"He probably doesn't want another puma to threaten him or us."

"Here, you have a pet jaguar, a wild one. Back in New Mexico I have a pet dog. Our lives sure are different. I doubt if any of my friends would believe you're real."

"You're adapting, though. In practically no time. Okay. Here's what we'll do. If we leave now, we can make my grandmother's village by tonight. If we get slowed down, we'll have to spend the night in the jungle. To be prepared for the worst, we'll each take a poncho along to sleep on. I've got two of them. Fill up these two canteens while I get some jerky."

Jake ducked through the undersized doorway, and headed straight to the stream. Chanti met him in front, weapons slung and sack of food and poncho tied at her back. She extended her hand with the red insect repellant and they both rubbed it into their exposed skin. Jake bent as he slipped inside to grab his weapons and his poncho. She started for the jungle when he returned, Ba lam loping ahead. Jake rushed to catch up.

Chanti led the way in a different direction than they'd gone before, swinging her machete to cut through the dense green. "We'll go through the jungle even though it's harder than the river. That way's too dangerous because of the kidnappers."

Ba lam vanished and they didn't see him again.

Jake noticed more details now that he felt more comfortable in the rain forest. The jungle suggested stillness in the early morning, but it was never still. When he jostled the saw grass, the deluge of ants, spiders and beetles made the hairs on his arms stand on end.

Soon the jungle pulsed with the sound of insects. A macaw screeched, wings flapped, mosquitoes swarmed. The red stuff kept most away.

Jake relieved Chanti with the machete. Two slashes of the blade cut the growth near the ground. Two more slashes high overhead caused the vegetation to flop down. The growth swarmed with ticks, mosquitoes and stinging bugs as he hacked away. Even the red stuff couldn't repel them all. He itched all over, but kept swinging the machete.

A pulpy fruit struck him on the shoulder. He whirled and searched the trees. Chanti smiled and watched. A parrot squawked and shuffled along a branch, perhaps amused by it all. Then he saw his attacker. A monkey chattered at him from a nearby tree.

"It's best not to mess with the monkeys. We're in their territory. If you threaten one, the males will circle you and spray you with urine," Chanti said. "Let's go a little further and stop for food."

"Good idea. I'm thirsty and hungry. Is there a McDonalds near?" Jake grinned, but Chanti only frowned.

"Sorry. You probably don't know what that is."

"No. I don't."

"Not important. I was trying to be funny."

A few minutes later, Chanti said, "I see breakfast. Be right back." She disappeared.

When she returned with several fruits, she slashed a couple open for breakfast.

"This is guiro. It looks strange with its black meat, but tastes good."

"Hey. It is pretty good. It tastes like cantaloupe." Jake gobbled down one and started on a second. They both sipped water, too, from their canteens.

"I don't know how you find your way through here. There're no visible land marks," Jake said.

Chanti's eyes sparkled and her mouth twitched. "Maybe we're lost. I've never come this exact way. Actually, I'm trying to hit the river up a ways. I hope we'll miss any kidnappers and the river'll take us to Grandma."

Chanti glanced toward the trail. Her mouth dropped open and she jumped to her feet.

"Up. Quick."

8

Chanti pointed to a swarm of ants racing toward them. "Fire ants. Time to move on. They're not much fun."

She led the way with her machete, hacking at the thickened foliage. Chanti's neck and shoulders glistened with sweat. Every so often, sunlight streaked through an opening in the green canopy and picked out the red highlights in her black hair.

As Jake followed, a powerful hissing noise behind him broke the silence. It vibrated like a rattle, but a hundred times faster than a rattlesnake. He turned.

Twelve feet long and as thick as his thigh, a ponderous chocolate brown boa constrictor closed on him, five feet away. Pale, sandy brown spots, some big and others smaller, camouflaged it.

It slid over the path he and Chanti had created, moving in a straight line, not fast, but steady. Startled, Jake stepped back. His heel caught on a log. He stumbled, feet flailing to find balance.

"Chanti," he called out in the middle of the fall. As he landed on his back, his breath whooshed out.

The boa, too close now, shot its head toward him. Jake's heels scrabbled in the earth as he tried to launch himself on his back away from the reptile.

The snake, its cavernous mouth wide open, hit Jake in the shoulder as he leaned his head out of the way. It bit hard.

Jake yelled, "Aaaargh."

Chanti's arm streaked down and her machete sliced through the boa's neck, severing the head from its thick body. The jaws remained clamped to Jake's shoulder.

Mouth open, eyes wide, he stared into the cold reptilian eyeballs as they dimmed.

"Arrgh. Get it off me," Jake screamed. His hands shook as he tried to pull the head off. He only bloodied them and tore the gashes open.

Chanti pried the jaws open using the machete. She threw the head into the brush. The twelve-foot body continued to writhe on the jungle floor for another minute. Jake shivered as if it were a winter day.

"It's a good thing you ducked your head. Sorry I couldn't get to you quicker." Her head turned as she searched the jungle. "There's something over there for your wounds. I'll get it. Boas aren't poisonous, but the bite could get infected."

Chanti strode to a nearby tree and slashed its trunk. She caught the milky liquid that oozed out in her hand and returned. "Sictelo. A good tree to remember," she explained. "It's used as medicine for jungle skin disease, but it'll work as a disinfectant, too."

"I can't believe I fell in front of that thing. It surprised me, but that's no excuse."

Chanti knelt, unbuttoned and pulled his shirt back. "Boa constrictors are ambush hunters. They kill by suffocating rather than crushing." She rubbed the milky substance into Jake's puncture wounds. "On the ground, they don't move too fast. Not like the fer-de-lance."

Jake let out a deep breath and his shoulders slumped forward.

"How do you feel?" She asked.

"Shaky, but okay. Thanks. I'm glad you were here. You were right about snakes. I guess I got sloppy, not seeing any for a while. I was looking for something else, like a puma."

"Don't worry. It's nothing serious. The Sictelo will help it heal. You'll probably be bothered more by a bruise than the punctures." They stood. "I'm going to show you something else that could be a lifesaver."

Chanti trotted to a gigantic tree. She pulled a vine so Jake could see it. "When you need water and there's no stream." Her machete again flashed in the light as she cut a five-foot section and held it to her mouth. Foam formed at the cut's end, followed by a stream of water. She swallowed mouthful after mouthful. Leveling the vine to stop the flow, she offered it to Jake. "It's safe to drink."

Jake took it, tilting it to his mouth and gulped the remainder. "It tastes like river water, cool and delicious. The jungle's like a huge market place, but you don't need money."

"Are you hungry?" Chanti asked.

"Yeah."

"We'll find something as we go."

Jake followed Chanti as she padded along, eyes darting side to side. She stopped in front of a small palm tree. With one stroke, she cut it down. She used her machete to peel the bark and cut out its soft heart, which she cut in half.

"The Lacandons call this Uatapil. I have no idea if there's an English equivalent. Eat it. It's good." She bit into her piece.

Jake took a bite, "Hey. Tastes like nuts. Not bad. Wouldn't have thought it had that much flavor."

Finished, Chanti pointed toward a slender tree twenty feet away. "That's cocoa." Its straight trunk wasn't any wider than Jake's mom's Mr. Coffee at home. As she arrived at the tree, she sheathed her machete, reached up to a limb and climbed monkey-style to the small yellow gourd-like fruit. Breaking off a half dozen, she threw them to Jake, "Catch."

The first one bounced off his chest, but he caught the rest. She dropped to the ground in seconds, withdrew her machete and hacked away the cocoa fruit's tough shell. She showed him the jelly-like substance around the seeds, dipped her fingers in and ate it. Jake tried some. "Tasty." After eating a couple mouthfuls more, Jake said, "I've had enough."

"The Lacandons bake the beans, grind them and put them in posole. You ever eaten posole?"

"Yeh, It's good. You make surviving in the jungle so easy. I'd probably starve to death or die of thirst without you. Not to mention end up going around in circles."

Chanti motioned for Jake to follow and they walked on, in single file. A few minutes later, they came out from dense vegetation onto a faint trail.

Chanti stopped. Jake came within inches of running into her and stepped back. She unslung her bow and withdrew an arrow. With an effortless movement, she fitted the arrow and drew the bowstring back. Her arms steady, it twanged as the arrow flew to its mark.

Twenty feet down the path, a gray snake no bigger around than his little finger writhed around the arrow, impaled.

"To the Lacandons, it's víbora, or viper. They're hard to see," Chanti said.

It looked like a dead branch. Unless it moved, Jake would never have seen it. She grabbed her machete from where she'd dropped it, strode to the squirming snake and lopped off its head. Slicing the snake's body to free her arrow, she wiped the projectile on a small tree's leaves and replaced it in her quiver.

"We should move on. We won't make the village by tonight at this rate."

Humbled by what happened, Jake knew he'd be dead several times if not for Chanti. He didn't know what to say, so he kept his mouth shut.

"We're getting close to the river. There's a faint trail you should be able to follow that ends up there. The going's easy. If you should lose the track, bear left toward the water. I'm going to head off here through the thick stuff and try to find a dugout I hid near here. You follow the path to the river and wait for me. Keep your eyes open and you'll be fine."

"Sounds good. I'll be okay." He watched as Chanti disappeared into the steamy vegetation. Alone, he felt abandoned. Scared, too, when he thought of all he depended on Chanti for. He rolled his sore shoulder a few times to loosen it. She was right. His injured shoulder ached. The snake had left a bruise. He focused on what he was doing and willed the pain away. Jake wandered down the indistinct trail. Nothing but rain forest.

What's that?

He turned to glance back the way he'd come. He wiped his slippery palms on his pants.

A soft noise.

From off to his left.

Jake's hands whipped his rifle up. His head turned side to side.

It sounded again.

A low rasping sigh.

Breathing, he thought. Like something catching in the throat in the middle of a breath.

Jake's finger tightened on his rifle's trigger. He faced the sound. It definitely came from the left, from somewhere behind the rocky, impenetrable jungle. He swallowed.

There's someone or something in there.

Gun up, ready, Jake zigzagged through the vegetation. He avoided breaking branches, or dragging them across his clothes, and stepping on anything that might snap.

He stopped, held his breath, waited.

There.

His head snapped right.

Again. The breathing sound. Louder, closer.

Jake slid between two gigantic chicle trees.

The sound came again from behind him. Jake spun, rifle ready in his sweat- slippery hands. Shadows everywhere.

A different sound. The soft pad of a foot or paw in the rotting vegetation.

He listened. It was hard to tell with his own heart pounding in his ears.

Could I have imagined all that? Whatever it was, it's gone now. This is silly. I've forgotten what I've learned since I met Chanti. Jake took some deep breaths, easing them out slowly, relaxing. *I'll think of this as fun. I can handle whatever it is.*

He took stock of where he'd walked the past few minutes. He'd moved in a circle.

Circling? Maybe it doubled back. Uh, oh. It's stalking me.

Jake spun in a half circle. Beads of sweat dripped from his forehead. He placed his back against a huge trunk.

Another, different sound. Running water. Behind the tree. He glanced over his shoulder through some foliage. A wide, deep stream looked cool and inviting.

He looked to the front.

His mouth dropped open.

9

"Oh, oh! There you are," Jake whispered.

The big tawny-yellow cat could be Ba lam's cousin, stocky, but weighed 250 or 300 pounds. His coat lightened to whitish on the throat and belly. The broad heavy head and neck sported small spots and its sides and flank, dark open rings. The jaguar's unblinking stare unnerved Jake.

I'll be okay. Snap out of it, Jake. Nobody'll ever believe this story.

Jake slid around the tree and jogged to the stream's edge. Turning, he faced the way he came. The jaguar stepped around the tree.

If I only wound him, he'll tear me apart. Besides, I don't want to kill him. It would be like killing Ba lam. Maybe I can lose him in the water.

He dropped his M14 and shell belt on the bank and backed into the stream. He kept his eyes locked on the big cat. The dark, tea-colored water rose to his waist. A couple more steps and it came to his neck.

The cat crouched on the bank, watching. It leaped.

Jake whirled and swam downstream.

The big jaguar smacked the water as if he'd done a cannon ball.

The water's surge hit Jake like a tidal wave. He willed his arms to go faster. He looked back to find he wasn't pulling away.

The jaguar drew closer.

Jake sucked in three large breaths, exhaling the first two, and dove to the sediment covered black bottom. He gazed back through dirty water as he breast stroked downstream. The big paws paddled right above his feet. Too close.

Although Jake didn't swim faster, the jaguar slowed to a stop. *Great. Never heard of a cat swimming underwater. Now, if he'll just get out of the water and leave.*

Jake swam until his lungs wanted to burst. He slipped to the far side of the stream and slid his head above water. Easing his breath out, he strained to breathe in silently. He looked back to the spot he'd entered the stream. The jaguar, shoulders bunched, leaped to the stream's bank, shook off a spray of water, nosed Jake's rifle and disappeared into the jungle.

Hey. I did it. Now, I'll wait a while to make sure he doesn't double back again. At least it's cool in the water. I could stay here all day.

Something rustled in the jungle. Monkeys shrieked their shrill cries. He shivered. *I don't like being here alone. Time to get moving and find Chanti.* He breast stroked back toward his rifle and shell belt, causing barely a ripple in the stream's surface. Head turning, his gaze darted in all directions. He paused twenty feet from the rifle, searching while he treaded water.

No sign of the jaguar, snakes or man. He dashed for shore in a few swift strokes, pushed himself out, grabbed his weapon and watched again.

The hair on Jake's arms stood on end. A dark, sinister rope-like body slithered silently along a huge limb above him. He stepped ten feet to the right, never taking his eyes off the boa. It hung with its head a foot above the ground, tail wrapped around the limb. Jake stumbled back several more feet. His shoulder ached as he lifted his rifle. *I'm ready this time. You'd better back off.*

Seeming to understand, the big snake pulled itself back to the limb and rested.

Jake studied his location for a moment. He figured out where the trail he'd been on lay when the jaguar stalked him. He threaded his way through the tight undergrowth. *I need a machete.*

Keen eyes scanned every cluster of underbrush and searched every tree branch. He reached the dim path and edged his way along the original direction. *I don't want to step on one of those víboras. They're hard to see. It's sure tough to watch all sides and above, too. The jungle is a dangerous place for newbies like me who don't know it. Oh, well. I'll just go slow.*

Jake picked up speed, his confidence returning after not seeing any danger for fifteen minutes. The water's coolness had disappeared. The steamy, humid atmosphere and his exertions parched his throat and lips. *My tongue even feels swollen. Maybe I can find one of those vines.* With the idea of finding a drink, he forgot the oppressive, perpetual dampness.

Spotting the right vine and licking his dry lips, he picked his way to it with care. Drawing his knife, he discovered it wasn't sharp like Chanti's machete. He sawed a five foot section off and drank every drop.

Heat.

Humidity enveloped him, sheathing him in rivulets of sweat. He'd no sooner finished his drink than thirst nagged him again.

Crouching on a sloping boulder, he studied the path before him. The faint trail descended into a narrow cleft, a jagged crevice no more than a football field long and steep on both sides.

He gazed down the trail and into the darkness. The overgrown path ended at an exposed rock, a darkened doorway. *Am I seeing things? Are those columns on either side of the entryway?* Loose soil and torn branches lay in heaps beside the archway. *It looks newly excavated. Maybe an old Maya ruin. There have to be people around. Maybe they're like the kidnappers. Where's Chanti? I better find her soon. Have to get to the river.*

Jake expelled a long breath and breathed deeply twice to release his tension. Already conditioned by the jungle to be wary, he listened for any distant sound or the slightest noise. His eyes searched the terrain for predators. . . human, animal or reptile.

In the shadows, he squatted on the rock, in silence, listening and watching. Nothing moved except the fluttering wings of a few scarlet macaws. His right hand and trigger finger ached from gripping the rifle.

Jake slid from the boulder, holding his rifle one handed, using his other to help the descent. Edging forward, his gaze darted everywhere, leaving nothing unexplored. He remembered to search the tree limbs, too. He prowled down the path, looking ahead or above, scanning the shadows. Only thick branches, floppy leaves and patches of blue revealed by holes in the forest's canopy revealed themselves. After 100 yards of careful steps, he stood before the dark, open archway. A musty, dead stench, along with a fresh earth smell, flowed from the opening.

He crouched ten feet from the entrance, trying to penetrate the stygian darkness. Nothing. No sound. Imbedded in the dust, several footprints angled in all directions.

Snap!

Jake whirled and lifted his rifle.

Nothing.

A tense breath escaped. Breathing hard, he steadied himself, searching the shadows. His shoulder still ached. The need to run nearly got the better of him. He scowled. *Quit acting like a child. Patience, Jake. Take it easy.*

The vague footpath led on past the entrance becoming a better-defined path. He followed it, tense with listening and watching. He shook his shoulders to relieve the tension. *I can do this. Nothing's going to stop me from getting to Chanti.* A smile grew on his lips and became a laugh. He stepped forward lightly and increased his speed a little. He continued to look to both sides, up and down, but his stride loosened up, became more fluid. Details grew clearer.

Jake edged around an overhanging limb with a fat boa poised on it. As he cleared the tree, the sound of rushing water hit his ears. He slowed his pace. *Whoever uncovered the ruin could be at the river.* He remembered Chanti's advice, "Condider everyone and everything an enemy until he's proven he's a friend." *I hope Chanti didn't run into trouble.* He slipped along the trail, hugging the right side. The water's rumble grew more distinct. As the path curved to the left, Jake paused and inched forward to peer around a huge chicle tree.

Fifty yards along the trail, Jake spotted two wooden boats equipped with outboard motors tied to a mangrove. He searched on all sides for sign of a human presence. No one. Nothing. *It's too quiet. No people, crocodiles, snakes.* He squatted under the tree, half hidden, rifle ready.

A small two-man dugout glided into view. Chanti. She used her paddle as a rudder and coasted toward the tied boats, head in constant motion as she searched for enemies. Jake stood and her gaze locked on him. His heart thudded against his chest when she smiled.

A faint sound and a glimpse of something with his peripheral vision signaled a movement behind him.

Jake wheeled to meet an attack, muscles tense.

10

The air whooshed from Jake's lungs.

"Ba lam. You scared me." He lowered his M14 and sucked in a deep breath. The big cat stood two feet from him, tail swishing, yellow eyes gleaming against his dark fur.

"How'd you get so close without me hearing you?" Jake reached out his hand for Ba lam to smell.

The jaguar licked it once, ducked around him and trotted toward Chanti. Just brushing against Jake's leg knocked him sideways. The latent power made Jake shiver. *I don't want to tangle one-on-one with the likes of you.* The image of the big jaguar hitting the puma in midair popped into his mind. *I'm glad your big yellow cousin didn't get a hold of me.*

Chanti pulled her dugout ashore twenty yards upriver from the motorboats as Ba lam bounded to her. He let her wrestle him to the ground amidst much snorting and growling from both. Ba lam pretended to yield. He purred as she sat on his chest, hands on either side of him, pushing his head side to side.

"Ah, Ba lam. You're getting too big. You could snap me in two."

"It's fun seeing you two wrestling together," Jake said. "It's amazing a wild animal that kills with such savagery will play like a kitten with you."

"It's because we were constant companions for months. I was his substitute mother, but he considered me the real thing. I saved his life many times and he's saved mine. We trust each other. It's not something anyone else can duplicate with him."

"He seems to accept me, or at least tolerate me. I hope he thinks of me as a friend," Jake said.

"Don't worry. How'd your trek go? Any trouble?"

"It worked out all right. I met one of Ba lam's brothers, but solved the problem with no bloodshed. Just up this trail, someone's uncovered some ruins. Maya, I guess. Those must be their boats." He pointed to the two motor launches. "I haven't seen anyone, though."

"Good. They're probably chicleros and grave robbers. Chicleros used to take the sap from the chicle trees used to make chewing gum, but it's become much more profitable for them to steal historical artifacts and sell them in Guatemala or Belize. Since there're so many undiscovered ruins around, they have lots of opportunities. They're thieves and some are killers. It's better not to meet any. But if I can ever stop them, or, at least slow their operation, I do it. They're stealing my grandma's heritage. Mine, too."

"Maybe we can explore the ruins?" Jake asked.

Ba lam wandered off again. Chanti stood for a moment.

"Okay. Let's hide my dugout and we'll see what's up."

Jake and Chanti dragged the dugout into some brush above the shoreline. Jake threw dead leaves and branches on it and Chanti wiped out the drag marks with a branch.

"Keep a sharp eye out for the thieves. They get nasty if they're caught," Chanti said.

Jake led the way up the trail, stalking, primed. Chanti followed a step behind, an arrow ready to draw back.

"Hold up a minute," Chanti said. "If we go into the ruins, we'll need torches. Here's a tree we can get sap from. Keep watch while I make a couple."

While Jake studied the jungle, Chanti hacked two torch-sized branches and slipped over to a large trunk where she slashed two long gouges. As the thick sap ran out, she held the torches under it, turning them, forming large knobs.

"We'll let it dry a little and harden. It'll burn for a couple of hours. See anything?"

"Nope. We seem to be alone. Even Ba lam's gone."

Chanti cleaned her machete in the dirt as they talked. "Let's head on up. By the time we get there, the torches'll be fine."

Jake set off at a fast pace toward the excavated ruins. The last twenty yards they slowed to a crawl. When they arrived in front of the columned entrance, they paused to listen. Nothing. They found hunting scenes carved into the outside columns. One image resembled a jaguar. They peered inside, but darkness covered everything. Jake stepped to the murky gateway while Chanti lit one torch.

"We'll use one torch now and keep the other in reserve. I'll lead with the light and you keep your M14 ready," Chanti whispered.

They slipped through the arch with brackets of stone used to support it. Once inside, the flickering light showed a row of whole pots and fragments lining the left side. Some of the pottery's surfaces appeared yellowish white and some cream-colored. All had figures drawn in black lines, people and animals.

"Wow. Look at this one." Jake lifted a well-preserved cream-colored pot with a drawing of a man in a large headdress, arms raised. "It looks like they just made it yesterday."

"Jake. Shhhh." Chanti had her finger to her lips. Squatting side by side, holding their breath, they listened. Nothing.

Moments later, they exhaled. "My imagination, I guess," Chanti said. But Jake had come to trust her instincts. He waited, silent. Still nothing.

"Maybe so. But let's be careful," he said.

As they glanced around, nothing special excited their interest. The undersized room contained a small stone bench or altar besides the pottery. Covered with dirt, its identity remained unknown. Centuries of dust coated the stone walls. Chanti poked her head through a doorway into another room.

"Look at this, Jake." She stepped in to allow Jake to enter. Here, the light danced over well-preserved wall murals, still colorful with lots of reds and oranges even though faded. Awestruck, they stared. The mural, perhaps four feet high, started a foot off the ground and wrapped around the walls. Painted for short-statured Mayas, Chanti and Jake needed to bend to see it closely. The scenes depicted war, torture and gory rituals. Jake pointed to a figure with a definite Maya nose.

"They haven't changed a bit. Look at this one with a jaguar-skin robe. How come they only wore them from the waist down?" Jake asked.

"No idea, unless because it was so hot and humid."

"These scenes sure are bloody. Look at this, they're beheading a prisoner as a sacrifice," Jake said.

"It seems to be part of a series. Here's a battle taking place with lots of blood. Then prisoners in front of a lord. Next, the captured prisoners prostrate before the king. Then the one you're looking at."

"Over here are men with white headdresses and necklaces, knobbed red and gold scepters with musicians and dancers parading in front of them."

A clang echoed through a second archway. Voices sounded far away, but moved closer. A faint light appeared.

"Quick," Chanti said. "Let's duck down that stairway." She pointed to a dark opening in the floor. "Maybe they'll leave and we can explore some more. I'll go first with the torch."

The light through the doorway grew brighter. The voices sounded a few feet away. Chanti dropped down a flight of irregular rough-cut steps into the darkness to a dank underground chamber with a high ceiling. Jake, following too close, stumbled once and steadied himself with a hand on her shoulder.

As they reached the bottom, Chanti whispered, "Look around quickly to get your bearings. I'm going to douse the light."

Before she put out the torch, they spotted the writhing mass in a depression beside the near wall, twenty feet from the steps.

"That can't be what I think it is," whispered Jake in the inky blackness.

"It is. Move over here." She pulled him by his arm to the other side of the stone steps.

"Will they come after us?"

"Not if you don't talk."

Lights flickered through the opening at the top of the steps.

"They're speaking Maya. Probably chicleros," Chanti whispered in his ear, hand still on his arm. Her breath in his ear and feathery touch sent goose bumps up and down his body.

What's wrong with me? Here we are in danger from above and a huge snake's nest a few feet away and I'm thinking about her.

A torchbearer stood at the opening above, looking down. They ducked back. Ten feet away, in the dim flickering light, a rope-like dark form slithered toward them.

"Uh, oh. Nauyaca," Chanti murmured. Her machete whispered as she slipped it from its sheath.

11

The torch-baring antiquities thief spewed some rapid fire Maya and vanished. Chanti handed Jake the matches. "Light one so we can see the snake, but don't light the torch yet."

Jake did. The serpent, two feet away, wriggled toward them. Chanti stepped forward, her arm blurred with the downward machete strike. The nauyaca's head fell to the stone floor. Blood spurted from the neck and the body squirmed and flopped. After a few moments, it stopped. The head's gaping jaws remained open, but the eyes had glazed over.

Jake yelped and dropped the match.

"Light this torch. The chicleros've gone. The one with the torch saw the snake and wanted no part of it."

Jake's hand met Chanti's. As he took it, an electrical pulse blazed through his hand. He struck another match and lit the torch.

"I wish I hadn't done that. Look what's coming now," Jake said, pointing at two more long shapes slithering in their direction. "Quick. Up the stairs."

They darted up the first six steps and paused to watch as the two nauyacas stopped at the stairway's base. The nearer one slithered onto the first step.

"I'm adding snakes to my list of scorpions and spiders," Jake said, grimacing.

Chanti smiled back. Her full lips parted and her eyes lit up. Jake had to look away. "You're doing okay. Just think what it would be like to fall into that slimy, squirming snake's nest." She teased Jake with a mischievous smile.

"Thanks. I needed that image. Now, I probably won't sleep tonight."

They turned and Chanti led the way up. Holding the torch below the opening's level, she poked her head above and peered around the upper room.

"All clear, but they're not far." She turned toward the door the grave robbers had come from and they prowled deeper into the ruins.

They discovered two more connected rooms. As they wandered through the first, torchlight flickered, casting moving shadows on the walls, floor and ceiling. Jake half expected an ancient Maya warrior to step from the gloom. He shuddered as he recalled every detail of one of the wall mural's most gruesome scenes.

A damp, rotten smell spread throughout the long closed ruins. Somewhere, water dripped. The torch's narrow range pushed back the gloom for only a few feet before the impenetrable darkness swallowed it. They crept along, protected from the dark by the thin bubble of light. It prevented Jake and Chanti from seeing much of the walls. They slipped through the entrance and stopped in the last room.

"This's where the pots came from," Chanti said, pointing to the excavation work done by the relic hunters. The piled earth, dug away from a huge mound in the back corner, exposed stacked pots still in place. "They'll be back and we're trapped here. We'd better get out if we can. I made a mistake going farther into the ruins."

She glided to the door and peered out. "Clear so far. Come on."

Jake, M14 at the ready, followed. Darkness covered the walkway they had taken to get there. "Maybe we can get into the jungle without being seen." *I wish we had time to examine this ruin some more. Maybe next time.*

Chanti and Jake broke into a trot. One minute later, they peeked out the ruin's entrance. The pots stacked in the first room had disappeared. Far down the trail, near the boats, they spotted movement.

"Quick," Chanti said. "Into the jungle."

Together they dashed across the trail and vanished into the dense rain forest. Thirty feet in, Chanti stopped. Jake ran into her. "Sorry."

"Let's watch from here. If we're still, they won't see us."

They squatted behind the thick undergrowth and made themselves as comfortable as possible for a long vigil. An hour later, they remained in the same spot.

At least when we're moving, there're things to think about other than the sweat pouring down and bugs crawling all over me.

"Chanti, let's get out of here. I can't stand this."

"Wait a few more minutes."

No sooner had she spoken than the chicleros hiked up the trail from the river. Jake counted five leading the way in a single file. They could have been five-foot quintuplets, followed by a larger, fatter edition. The five, wearing huaraches and tattered, filthy white trousers and shirts, carried rifles and machetes. The big, mustachioed thief bringing up the rear, clad in rundown boots, sweat soaked khakis and a safari hat, had a holstered pistol strapped to his side. The once white handkerchief in his hand constantly wiped the sweat from his face.

"I've seen the big one before. He's a notorious thief. When they go inside, let's sink their boats and escape downriver in mine," Chanti said. "If things get out of hand and we have to run, head straight through the jungle to the river."

They remained silent as the six men drew abreast of their hiding place. Even without a breeze, the foul odor of long unwashed bodies drifted to them through the jungle's denseness.

The stocky lead man paused and looked straight at them. Jake stopped breathing. His hands gripped his rifle so hard he thought it might break.

The grimy relic thief looked down and stared at the spot they had entered the vegetation.

Uh, oh. You must see our tracks.

Knowing they couldn't run without getting shot, he inhaled and exhaled several deep, noiseless breaths. Jake's heart quit pounding so hard. He smiled to himself. *I'm ready.* His hands and trigger finger relaxed, but remained ready.

The fat man in the rear said something. The lead man shrugged and pivoted toward the ruins. He led the single-file trek to the entrance. They lit the three torches leaning against the wall and disappeared into the ruin's first room.

"Let's get my boat in the water," Chanti whispered. "We'll go through the jungle instead of by the trail where they might see us."

"That was close. If the fat one hadn't said something, I think the point man would have figured out we're here."

Chanti used her machete to break a path toward the river. They reached a place where the rain forest thinned allowing their pace to quicken to Chanti's hidden dugout. Uncovering it, they dragged it into the river and boarded. Once they arrived at the relic thieve's boats, they pulled into shore.

Chanti jumped into knee-deep water. She untied the two boats and pushed them into the river. Clambering aboard the nearest one, she stabbed her machete into the bottom several times to open big holes. Jumping out, she pushed the fast-sinking boat toward the river's center and boosted herself into the second. Repeating the process, she again leaped into the water and pushed. Jake maneuvered the dugout to her side and she bounded aboard. The whole event took two minutes.

A shout from shore. Their paddles stroked deep to propel them away. Jake glanced back to the antiquity hunters' stocky lead man. At the same time, the second ruptured boat sank. The man lifted his rifle and aimed.

"Duck," Jake said as he flattened himself as low as possible. Chanti did the same. A shot fired. The bullet splashed to the right. They dug their paddles in. The dugout flew down the river, caught in the current.

The rifle discharged again. Thunk into the dugout's side.

Twenty feet from a curve in the river.

Ten.

As they cut left, the rifle went off a last time. The bullet didn't come close. Chanti in the bow and Jake aft kept their paddles flying to put as much distance between them and the thieves as possible.

The river narrowed into a channel beneath the mangrove trees. White water gushed around large, jagged boulders. Submerged tree trunks extended branches high above the water, blocking passage. Jake and Chanti ducked to keep from ramming their heads on the snake-infested branches near shore. He used his paddle as a rudder and guided them to the river's center.

Jake paused in his paddling, his attention caught by something moving across the river. At first, it looked like a curved branch. He studied it and recognized the Barba Amarilla's yellow chin.

It streaked through the water.

"Chanti," Jake called. She saw it.

Her machete sparkled in a ray of sunlight. The snake, a variety of the Nauyaca, surged forward. It hooked its curved fangs on the dugout's side.

Only a foot from Jake, the dead eyes in its flat head locked on his. He whacked its head with his paddle. Nothing.

Chanti twisted in the dugout. "Keep us off the rocks," she said.

The machete saved them again as it slashed down, thunking into the wooden side. The long body fell away. She pried the jaws off the wood and flipped the head into the river.

The dugout streaked straight toward a saw-toothed rock jutting from the whitewater. Sweat poured off Jake's face. He strained every muscle to bring the boat to the right.

Chanti jammed her machete into its sheath, grabbed her paddle and joined the struggle. They yanked their paddles away as the dugout's left side scraped along the rock.

The river widened again and calmed.

"Phew. Close call," Jake's voice shook. Adrenaline had kept his focus in the middle of the action, but now that it had ended, his stomach churned and he trembled. He gulped several deep breaths.

"Thanks for keeping us off the rocks. It's hard to do two things at once when they're both life threatening." Her head was turned and her compliment and smile warmed his heart.

"Oh, no," Jake said, looking downriver past Chanti.   "Not   again."

12

A hundred yards downriver, a large canoe struggled against the current. Jake recognized the two paddlers and the powerful Indian resting in the middle. Kidnappers. The Indian "jefe" raised his rifle and sighted toward Chanti.

No place to go. Jake looked around, wildly.

"Steer," Jake blurted.

He, too, had raised his rifle. Their dugout cruised smoothly with the current. The kidnapper's dugout strained against the flow, buffeted about when not pointed straight into the current. The kidnapper boss fired first, but the bullet was off its mark. Jake shot over Chanti's near prone body. The paddler in the canoe's bow flopped back into the rifleman, dropping his paddle overboard.

"Watch out, Jake," Chanti said, peering over the boat's side, trying to keep the dugout's path steady.

Jake's finger already squeezed the trigger, front sight lined up on the rear paddler, who had paused and was aiming his rifle. The jefe waited behind the dead one. Jake's M14 cracked. The paddler in the stern pitched from the boat into the river.

"Look out, Jake." The one with the rifle tried to aim it over the other's shoulder.

Jeez. Won't this ever end?

Jake aimed at the part of the man's face that peaked from behind the other's head. He fired. The bullet thudded into the already dead man's forehead. It splattered pink and gray matter all over the boss man's face. He shoved the dead man off him and belly-flopped over the canoe's far side.

Already a large reptilian head approached the dead paddler floating twenty feet behind the dugout. Mouth wide open it hit the body, rolling over several times and vanishing into the deep. Another croc slid over the muddy bank into the river. It disappeared under the surface.

"Let's get that guy out of there," Chanti said. "That's no way for a man to die."

They both dipped deep with their paddles and the dugout flew the remaining fifty yards. The kidnapper clung to his dugout. He struggled to pull himself over the side without tipping it. The crocodile approached only feet away. Frantic, he capsized the boat. Still trying to pull himself up, his hands slipped from the smooth wet bottom.

Jake and Chanti swooped up between the croc and the man. Jake did a quick switch, dropping his paddle and snatching his M14. He shot down into one of the croc's bulging eyes. It floated there for a moment, the eye shattered, its gaping jaws still open. Then it sank, disappearing from sight several feet down.

Chanti spoke to the Indian. She held out her hand, leaned back and he pulled himself into the dugout as Jake steadied it. He lay there in the bow facing them, gasping for breath. His weapon had sunk to the river's bottom.

"Gracias. Gracias," he said hoarsely between gasps. He rattled off a flood of Spanish Jake couldn't follow. Chanti answered him.

"He wanted to know why we helped him when he would have killed us. I told him crocodiles are no way to die and we basically have no quarrel with him."

The man wasn't so fearful without his scowl and his weapon. Gone was the fierce, hostile stare from the bus. His attitude had changed. But he had muscles upon muscles, large knotted Popeye forearms. Even his facial muscles constantly bunched and unclenched as he spoke.

As Chanti and the kidnapper talked again, Jake recognized, "Me llamo Andrónico de la Cruz," and Chanti's response with both their names.

Jake stuck out his hand prepared for a crushing grip, but Andrónico didn't try to assert himself. He gave a firm handshake, nothing more. Chanti, too, shook his hand. *Hey, I don't seem to be mad at him, or bitter. Just happy I don't have to worry about him any more.*

After more rapid fire exchange of Spanish, Chanti said, "Andrónico apologizes for all the trouble he caused us both. He says he guesses he'll go back to farming. His kidnapping career is over. He got his whole gang killed. He wants to know if there's anything he can do to make up for what he's done."

"I'll think about it. Hey, let's stop his canoe before it gets away and grab at least one paddle," Jake said. "We don't want to keep him with us."

They swung their boat to pick up both paddles and get a hold on the capsized dugout. Andrónico grabbed the boat's bow and they towed it to shore. After beaching their own dugout, the three of them flipped the capsized canoe and dragged it alongside.

"Which way will he go? Jake asked.

"He needs to go way up river. It'll be a hard trip for one person in such a heavy dugout. Good thing he's so strong."

Crack.

Jake and Chanti whirled, facing upriver. Andrónico responded, but slower.

Snap. Something broke branches. The sharp sounds rose above the river's rushing water.

Chanti pointed. Her sharp eyes detected men working their way along the shore. They edged through the underbrush and mangroves along the river's edge. They had passed around the river's curve and struggled through the dense growth 100 yards away.

Jake counted six. The antiquity thieves. The same stocky point man led them now. He resembled Andrónico, but not as muscular. The fat mustachioed thief still trailed behind, struggling to keep pace, not a dry spot on his clothes.

"We can get out of here in our dugout, but that won't help Andrónico," Jake said. "Better explain to him what our problem is with them."

Chanti rattled off a lot of Spanish to him. His eyes grew larger when he understood. He answered her.

"He says he'll go with us for a ways. He's in no hurry and has no weapon. Okay with you?"

"Sure. Let's get started. They haven't seen us yet. Can he handle his boat alone?"

Chanti asked him. "He says so, going with the current."

As they splashed into the water and pushed their canoes out into the current, a shout echoed down to them from the chicleros. A shot sounded, but came nowhere near. Glancing back, Jake spotted the husky point man with his rifle up. He fired again, with the same result.

"Glad he's such a poor shot," Jake said, pulling hard on his paddle. The combination of their fast moving paddles and the strong current swept them from danger. They soon rounded another bend in the river. Twenty yards in front of Andrónico, they quit paddling and kept to the middle of the waterway. He drew alongside.

Chanti spoke rapidly to him, pointing to an inlet on the river's other side. "I told him he should hide out over there until they've passed. Then he can continue on his way upriver and head home."

Andrónico spoke again. "He says to thank you for saving his life. You're a warrior despite being so young. He's going back to his family and farm. Material things aren't that important."

The three of them exchanged handshakes for the last time. Chanti and Jake paddled downriver while Andrónico headed across to the inlet made by a stream emptying into the river. Jake glanced back to see him disappear up stream. *I should hate that guy for disrupting my life. I'm not sad he's gone, but he wasn't all bad. I guess I've led a pretty sheltered life and've never run into so many desperate poor people before. They must've seen kidnapping as a quick fix.*

"Can we get to your grandma's village on the river?"

"Almost. We'll have to paddle up a stream a short ways. We've lost so much time, we're going to stop. It'll be dark soon. The first likely looking spot we see, we'll head in."

As they glided down the widened river, birds swooped everywhere, gobbling up insects.

Bats joined them. The jungle's canopy cast broad shadows. Along the shore, a crocodile slid into the water. It headed toward them, but vanished beneath the river's surface before it reached them.

At last, Jake spotted a short stretch of stony beach. Chanti aimed the dugout at it. They beached the dugout and leaped onto the muddy slope.

"It'll be uncomfortable, but safer if we sleep in the dugout. Let's cut some branches to lay our ponchos on. We can make it fairly comfortable," Chanti said.

They rigged it so they'd be facing each other, backs against the opposite ends. Half the poncho would be under them, the other half pulled across the top. It protected them against the bugs as well as the rain. Chanti got out the red repellant and they put a good coat on their exposed skin. They ate some jerky with the last of the light. She had brought the two torches and lit the half used one, jamming it into the pebbled ground. They stretched out on their ponchos.

"Too bad Ba lam isn't here to guard us," Jake said.

"He could be somewhere near."

"How do you move through the jungle so quietly. I try, but I always snap a twig or rub against stuff."

"You probably concentrate on the pattern of bushes and trees right in front of you. You have to focus on the jungle further out and find breaks in the foliage. Look through the jungle, not at it. Once in a while, stop and stoop down to look along the jungle floor. You might see game trails you can follow."

"When I made that trek by myself, I grabbed a vine when I was climbing a slope. It had sharp thorns," Jake said.

"Don't grab bushes or vines. Lots of them have spines or thorns. Use a stick to part the vegetation. It'll help dislodge biting ants, spiders or snakes. I use my machete."

The night filled with deafening jarring sounds. Monkeys, birds, the cough of a jaguar grated on Jake's nerves. Something screamed. The torch burned out.

"This won't be like in my camp. There're so many creatures about, one of us will have to be awake all the time. I'll take the first watch. We'll switch every two hours. The worst danger'll come from the scorpions and the second worst'll be snakes. Look into the jungle. Under the triple canopy there's a faint light. It'll help us see in the dark."

"Where's it come from? I didn't see it before."

"It's some kind of glowing phosphorous in the dead vegetation on the jungle floor. It's not bright like the torch, but you can see animals or people fifty feet away. It's pretty. And maybe a little eerie."

"I'm so tired, even this noise can't keep me awake," Jake said. He slept fitfully. The pounding rain on their ponchos kept Jake awake for an hour. Thunder cracked like a giant whip. Lightning lit up the sky. Because of the canopy, Jake witnessed the light flashes, but only one jagged double strike flashed over the river.

They switched the watch every two hours through the night.

Jake had fallen asleep on the last watch. As the sky lightened, a loud roar woke them. It sounded huge. It grew louder and another roaring started on the other side of them. *What is it? Sounds like a lion, but we're not in Africa. Something's creeping up on us. They sound close enough to pounce and that'll be the end. But jaguars don't roar. Maybe pumas?*

13

"Those are only Howlers," Chanti eased his tension.

In the nearby trees, black shapes leaped through the branches. Because of their dark color and the trees' shadows, Jake couldn't make out details of their faces and bodies. He breathed a sigh of relief, amazed that a monkey could make such a savage howl.

"I've heard them before, but never this close. Half asleep, all I could think of was lions. I imagined lions or jaguars creeping up on us in the dark and, at any moment, they would pounce and that would be the end. Now I remember jaguars don't roar." Jake struggled to climb out of the dugout. "I'm an old man after sleeping in that thing all night. I can hardly straighten up."

Chanti's eyes widened. "Jake. Watch out. Look behind you."

Jake spun and looked into the gaping maw of a crocodile, huge dripping head still half in the water.

It burst from the river, sprinting toward him. Its hide glistened as the water rolled off. Huge teeth froze Jake for a moment.

He dodged aside toward the canoe. Bending, he scooped his rifle from the dugout's deck and jumped onto the river bank.

The crocodile switched directions, heading for him.

Jake ran ten yards and turned. The gator closed on him.

He threw his M14 to his shoulder and fired into the open throat.

It kept coming.

He fired the rest of the clip as fast as he could pull the trigger.

It stopped moving, seeming to deflate, its jaws sagged shut as its body collapsed to the jungle floor. The light in its eyes dimmed and went out.

Chanti stood two feet away, machete in hand. Relief showed in her softened expression before dissolving back to her usual deadpan.

"Wow. I didn't know they could move that fast."

"Good reflexes. I'm glad you're so quick. It's about fourteen feet. Big enough to eat you." She touched his hand. "But I'm happy it didn't." She was not made of steel. There was the hard and soft. A piratical sparkle gleamed in her eyes.

Now that it's over, my leg're wobbly. I wonder if she gets that way. I'd be embarrassed to ask her, though. She always seems so fearless.

"Better reload your clip," Chanti said.

Jake trudged back to the dugout, grabbed his shell belt, reloaded the 20-round clip and slammed it back into the weapon, racking the slide to shove one into the chamber. Chanti stood close beside him. It still amazed him that she moved like a shadow.

Her mouth spread in a bewitching smile. "You've learned fast, but you were careless there, not paying attention before you got out of the boat. It's strange, but I was scared for you and I almost never am for myself. I guess I like you and don't want to lose you." She took his hand and led him toward a fallen tree trunk. "Let's sit for a while. I love this time of day."

The morning mist hung over the river and in the trees, giving everything a magical quality. Jake continued to hold her hand.

Does she know I feel shaky and need to sit down? He smiled at the thought that she liked him and he forgot his shakiness. Jake looked up. *This rain forest is another world. It's got its own ceiling more than a hundred feet up.* The crowns of the trees interlocked and a lush matting of vines and giant ferns intermingled. *It's like a great green cavern.* Scarlet, indigo and emerald green flashed by as the parrots and parakeets darted from vine to tree fern.

"I see why you like it so much. If we only didn't have kidnappers and chicleros to worry about. Right now it's so peaceful and beautiful and just a few minutes ago I was almost eaten alive. But it's hard to stay alert in all this beauty."

"Maybe it'll help to imagine those big croc teeth biting into you."

"I'd be a lot more worried if I didn't have this." Jake raised his M14. "Could you have killed that croc with your machete if I'd missed?"

"Maybe."

Jake shuddered and looked at the beast.

A stick snapped. Chanti rose and in three strides, snatched up her bow and arrows. Only a second behind, Jake crouched, M14 ready.

Jake peered into the jungle through the undergrowth. Beside the canoe, Chanti drew an arrow halfway back, eyes scanning every tree and hidden corner. Together, as silently as Ba lam, they glided to the green wall. Not a twig cracked beneath their feet.

They crept into the rain forest. The foul odor of unwashed bodies warned them of human closeness. Past the undergrowth, dark forms slipped through the thick jungle. The unclear shapes emerged as six men headed straight between Jake and Chanti.

Jake recognized the stocky lead man of the grave robbers. Behind him trudged four more short chicleros and the large, fat mustachioed thief brought up the rear. The five carried rifles and the big man clutched a pistol.

What now? They probably heard me shooting the croc. If they get to the river, they'll see our boat. Better to face them here.

The point man surprised him. His steady gaze locked on Jake crouched beside a huge cedar tree. His mouth twisted, lips drawn back. His rifle flew to his shoulder, aimed straight at Jake.

An arrow blossomed from the chiclero's chest. He looked down. His eyes widened and his mouth dropped open before he pitched forward onto his face.

An instant later, knowing they were committed now, Jake aimed at the mustachioed leader in the rear. The man wiped his sweat-covered face with his discolored handkerchief, still unaware of what had happened up front.

The moment Jake's rifle cracked, the Indian in front of the boss chiclero stepped the wrong way. Right into the path of Jake's bullet. His head exploded onto the large man's face and chest.

Another arrow thunked into the arm of the second thief as all four dropped to the jungle floor and opened fire. They fired wildly since not one of them had seen either Jake or Chanti. Jake glanced over to where Chanti stood behind an immense mahogany tree.

She motioned him to follow as she sprinted toward her dugout. They flew over the open ground and reached the boat in seconds. Throwing everything in, they shoved off into the river.

Chanti jumped in the bow and after another push, Jake thrust himself into the stern. They plunged their paddles deep. The canoe reacted like a racehorse bursting from the starting gate.

Jake marveled at the rippling muscles in his friend's back and shoulders. She never paused and he matched her stroke for stroke. *I'm glad I'm in good shape so I can keep up with her. It sure would be embarrassing not to be able to.*

In moments they traveled 100 yards to a bend in the river and swept around it.

Safe. At least for now. They coasted. The four remaining chicleros probably still lay on the jungle floor.

As Jake looked toward shore, something dark passed between two trees. Only a glimpse.

I don't know if I saw something or it was my imagination. He stared hard. Nothing.

"I saw it, too," Chanti whispered loud enough so he could hear her over the gurgling river.

Jake gave his peripheral vision a chance by looking off to the side of where he'd seen it.

Thirty feet past the spot, it showed again. Big, black. Yellow eyes glittering. Watching them.

"It's Ba lam," Chanti said at the same time Jake thought of him.

"Let's head into shore," Jake said, dipping his paddle into the river.

Ba lam prowled under a large kapok tree as they closed in on land. Intent on guiding the canoe to a safe spot on shore, Jake saw something large drop from the tree onto the big cat from the corner of his eye.

"Boa," Chanti bellowed and dug her paddle in with all her strength. Jake added his back and arms to it and they beached the dugout in seconds.

The boa, a saddle-pattern coloration, dark brown with circular cream spots, had attached itself to Ba lam's bucking, twisting body. Its expandable jaws with large curved teeth locked on Ba lam's head. It wrapped its thick body around the jaguar, squeezing, trying to suffocate him.

They thrashed around in the brush amidst bloodthirsty growls and snarls. Ba lam staggered out to the shoreline, frantic, unable to shake it off. The two of them pitched into the river where boas thrive.

Chanti waded into the water, machete raised. Jake slogged in beside her, knife in hand. There was no possibility of shooting. Too risky.

"Hurry. The snake'll try to drown him," It was the first time Jake had heard panic in her voice. Chanti looked for an opening but the powerful cat turned and bucked, jaws snapping. He let out a thunderous scream.

The explosions of water cascading over them drenched Jake and Chanti. The eruptions from the river slowed. Ba lam's head stayed under the river's surface.

14

The instant the thrashing paused, Chanti and Jake moved to either side of the tangled up fighters. Jake slashed deep into the boa's thick coils which wrapped around Ba lam. Careful not to cut into the big cat, he ripped open the snake's body.

Chanti sawed with her machete to behead the huge constrictor. She stopped the blade before it sliced into Ba lam's still submerged neck and head.

"Hold his head up," Chanti's voice rose, almost to a scream.

Jake sheathed his knife and used both arms to lift Ba lam's big head from the river. The boa's jaws stayed fastened to it. The snake's upper jaw covered one eye, but the other gleamed at Jake. Wheezing, the jaguar sucked in small labored breaths.

Chanti's machete and hands ripped the boa's head from Ba lam and threw it on the stone-covered shoreline. Jake dragged the jaguar and the boa's lifeless body through the buoyant water toward shore. Chanti helped lift the jaguar onto dry land. The snake's coils must have relaxed in death, because Ba lam now gulped deep breaths. He stood on shaky legs. Jake and Chanti peeled the coiled, bloody body from the cat and threw it to the jungle floor..

Chanti swung her machete again and again, moaning, chopping up the boa.

"Chanti stop. Ba lam's okay."

She didn't respond. Jake ducked under the blade and wrapped his arms around her.

"He's all right. Stop."

Chanti leaned into Jake, resting her head on his chest. He could feel her shaking. He repeated over and over everything was okay. After a few moments, she calmed down.

Ba lam shook himself. Chanti hugged her black friend. "Even a jaguar has to pay attention. He was watching us instead of his surroundings," she said, a catch in her voice. "Sorry to lose it like that. It's the closest I've ever come to losing him. I feel weak, now. My legs want to give out." Ba lam's big tongue lapped her face. "Boas are great in the water and often drown their victims. This one must've been really hungry. Ba lam's too big for it, but it almost killed him. Let's see how long it is."

They stretched it out and added its head. Jake paced it off.

"About fourteen and a half feet. And I bet it weighs half as much as Ba lam. Is that big?"

"It's giant. I've never seen one like this. Half this size is common. Ten or twelve feet is large."

Ba lam purred now. Chanti kneeled close to him.

The cat rubbed his head against Chanti's rib cage.

"He saved you and now you've saved him."

"I'd have had trouble without you. He might have drowned."

Jake rubbed Ba lam's head. The yellow eyes turned to him. He purred louder.

"He likes you. He knows he was lucky. I've never known him to travel this far from our home territory."

"Maybe he's been following you," Jake said.

Ba lam padded on steady legs to the river and drank.

"Look at him. Just another day at the office," Jake said. "We'd better pay attention to those chicleros. We aren't very far from where we left them. I'll take a look upriver while you check out Ba lam."

"Thanks. Be careful." Chanti seemed subdued, not her usual unbreakable self.

Jake touched her shoulder and jogged to the jungle's edge. *As tough as she is, she cares. I'm glad he's okay because he's such an awesome animal and friend, but also, his death would really hurt Chanti.*

Jake slid into the dense jungle and stopped in a shadowed hollow, quelling his feelings for Ba lam and Chanti for now. Motionless, he watched. And listened. M14 ready.

Fifty yards upriver something moved. *Can't we have a few moments peace? Maybe it was nothing. I don't see any more movement.* This time a tapir pushed its way through the brush to the riverbank and drank. *Phew. Glad it's not the grave robbers.*

He watched again. Jake jumped when Chanti touched his arm.

"Wow. You scared me." The battering in his chest slowed to a mild throbbing. Calm returned. "How's Ba lam?"

"Fine. He's the same if he wakes up from a nap or fights a deadly battle. I hope he learned something from this one."

"No sign of chicleros."

"Let's get cleaned up in the river. We've both got blood and gore all over us," Chanti said.

Jake cast a final glance into the jungle and followed her to the river. Ba lam joined them in the water. He stood like a big dog, head up, letting her clean him.

As Chanti and Jake rinsed their clothes, she looked at him. "I'm going through the jungle with Ba lam and try to get him to go back to his own territory. You take the boat to the village and I'll meet you there. Are you okay with that?"

"Sure. Too bad we can't teach him to ride in a dugout." Jake wasn't sure how he felt about finding his way alone. He thought he'd probably be okay on the river, but he remembered how he never seemed to know where he was when going through the jungle. *I made it that time when I ran into Ba lam's yellow buddy, though.*

"About a mile downriver, a smaller river empties into this one from this side. Go upriver there about half a mile and you'll find some docks on the right. There's a well beaten path that'll take you to Grandma María's village."

"That won't be a problem." *I won't let her know I have any doubts. Suck it up, Jake. Quit being a baby.*

"There is one spot that could be treacherous. Be careful. There's white water that runs pretty fast and rough. If I didn't think you could make it, I wouldn't tell you to try. It's a place Mom and Dad loved to go through."

"I guess I might as well start, " Jake said. He rubbed Ba lam's forehead. "See you, Big Guy."

"Be careful. Nothing's changed. The jungle's still dangerous." Chanti stood on the bank with Ba lam.

Jake shoved the canoe out and slipped into it, grabbing a paddle. His rifle was slung across his back. He looked back and raised his hand. She and Ba lam stood watching. Chanti returned his salute.

I hope she'll be safe. Those chicleros keep showing up.

He paddled faster because he hadn't hit the smaller river yet. A low rumble sounded in the distance. The boat picked up speed even though he didn't dip his paddle into the river. The water squeezed into the mouth of a narrow canyon. The air was cooler than before and damp with haze. *Uh, oh. This is what Chanti was talking about. Look at that whitewater. The beginning of the canyon looks like a chute.*

It forced the untamed river to change to a torrent as it swept into a pinched chasm, forty feet wide. Within moments, the rumble changed to a roar. Through the mist, white foam shot over points of black, shiny rocks.

Jake gasped as he rocketed down the chute. "Yeee-haaw."

The perpendicular flat walls, with a sheen of polished marble, rose straight up to a thousand feet above the tumbling water. Jake didn't have time to appreciate the beauty. He needed every bit of his skill to keep the dugout upright as the wild current shot him straight through the menacing gorge. Once more he screamed in exhilaration.

Biting his lip and paddling first on one side, then the other, he avoided several small boulders. A large one stood in the gorge's center and required all his strength to sweep around it. Groaning, he plunged his paddle deep, using his whole body. He thought for a moment he'd have to push away from it with his paddle, but he cleared it with inches to spare.

He guided the canoe to the canyon's end with no mishap. Any capsize in this ominous cleft of skyscraper rock walls would have dumped him into the river for a long, dangerous swim. The sheer walls offered nothing to hang onto. *With all the nasty creatures I've seen in this river, I don't want to go swimming.*

As he popped out of the canyon, he relaxed. *Wow. That's the wildest ride I ever took.* His chin slumped to his chest. He took a couple of deep breaths.

Too close to the river's edge, the strong current took control and the boat careened into a thorn patch hanging over the bank. Blood gushed from his forehead and arms. The thorns were half an inch thick and two inches long. *Man. The jungle doesn't let up for a second.*

Besides the thorns, the bugs, heat and tree-hanging snakes were a constant threat. He piloted the canoe well offshore to avoid another mishap.

At last. The other river. Jake turned. Now paddling upriver, he put his back into it. Exhausted from the whitewater, his arms quivered. Both sides of this river were covered with rocky, impenetrable jungle that seemed to be infested by all the snakes in the world.

Keeping a sharp eye on the low, overhanging tree branches, Jake kept a steady pace.

The jungle thinned out. The riverbanks no longer hid beneath dense growth. A parrot squawked and shuffled along an overhanging branch.

On a high bank, set back about fifty feet, stood a lone hut. It resembled Chanti's. Close to the river walked a solitary figure. An aged woman with deep wrinkles. She was a replica of an ancient Maya. High cheekbones, slanted back forehead, obsidian eyes; the same face that confronted the Spanish Conquistadores almost 500 years ago. She stared at Jake as he glided by, and he at her. He waved, but drew no response.

A cornfield showed through the trees. *All right. Civilization at last. What am I happy about? I might have to leave Chanti.*

Two tumbledown ancient docks jutted out into the water. Three battered dugouts were tied to the first and an outboard motor-propelled skiff to the second. Jake eased his canoe into the second on the opposite side from the skiff.

A half dozen teenage Lacandons, all hooded by shoulder-length hair and wearing old jeans or army fatigues, advanced from the trees.

"Chanti's boat," said the leader, waving his machete.

15

The slim Lacondon leader wore Levis and jacket with no shirt and on his feet, battered huaraches. Besides the machete he twirled in his hand, he carried a 22 rifle slung over his left shoulder, barrel down. His wide mouth grimaced in a perpetual scowl.

He's somewhere around my age or Chanti's and not as tall as her. None of these guys are very big.

When Jake stood in the wobbly dugout, he steadied himself with a hand on the wharf. He picked up the M14 and held it ready as he stepped up to the dock. The Lacondons stopped advancing. Several took a step back.

The Indian leader, unphased by the weapon, stepped toward Jake again. "Where Chanti?"

"I'm to meet her here. She's coming through the jungle," Jake said.

"We swap rifles. I take yours. Give to Chan Kin."

"No. I don't think so."

"I need. You buy other rifle. Chan Kin have no money. You have money. Give me rifle."

"I need it, too." *At least he isn't threatening me. But he sure has no inhibitions about asking. Glad he speaks a little English. I know I'm an intruder. Hope Chanti gets here soon.*

"Why you red?" Chan Kin asked.

"To keep away insects. Chanti's idea."

"Chanti smart. She know all about jungle. How you meet?"

"I was kidnapped off a bus and escaped. She helped me when I got to the jungle. Saved my life," Jake said, the tenseness draining from his body. "Can I get to her Grandma María's on that path?" He pointed to the trampled path beneath the two hundred foot mahogany trees leading away from the river.

"Yes. Chan Kin help you, friend of Chanti." He spoke in rapid Lacandon to his five friends. Pivoting, they headed up the path. Jake grabbed his belongings from the dugout and followed. Chan Kin looked back slyly, "Then you give big gun."

"I'll tell you what. When I leave the jungle to go home, if Chanti doesn't want it, I'll give it to you. Okay?"

Chan Kin nodded like he had just been given a tortilla at dinner. He walked with a slight swagger, though. Jake thought he caught a glimpse of a faint smile on his profile as he turned back up the path. He followed the Indians through a cornfield and back into the forest. Bananas ripened and scented the air. They hiked the zigzag path to the village. Along the way, two teenage boys beat an armadillo into submission with clubs.

As they approached the huts, barking dogs nipped at their heels and dwarf-like children with huge round eyes turned to stare at him. Chan Kin pointed out María's hut. It was eight feet long, ten feet wide and a little over five feet high, spacious in comparison to many of the other twenty huts of the Lacanja community, but just as primitive. Built on poles with no walls, the huts drooped with musty thatched-roofs that hung over the sides low enough to give some privacy and smelled of wood smoke and moist earth.

His Indian guides halted at an open hut next to María's. Several Lacandons, all with shoulder length black hair, sat cross-legged on the floor. A ten-year old little girl leaned against the back wall and puffed on a cigar. Some of the Indians wore homespun cotton robes, but others wore blue jeans and shirts or old army fatigues.

Crescent bananas, spiral roots and corn dangled from the rafters like objects in a still-life painting. An old woman squatted by the fire and slowly rolled cigars. Flames reflected in her dark eyes. A young woman lay in a hammock nursing a child while an older, plump woman sat on a stack of folded mosquito netting and smoked a cigar. A boy stood in the corner feeding a spider monkey.

"Jake." Chanti strolled up. "Hello, Chan Kin. Are you helping my friend, Jake?" Chanti said.

"Chan Kin met me at the dock," Jake said.

"Yaake give me big rifle when he leave jungle."

"I said if Chanti doesn't want it."

"Chan Kin," Chanti said. "It's Juh-Jake. Almost like Chuh in Chan or Chanti. We'll see you later. Thanks for helping Jake. I want him to meet María, now."

Chanti took Jake's arm and headed to the next hut. A warmth spread through him when she pressed into his arm.

"My grandma's only fifty years old. Still pretty young."

María stood in the middle of the hut. She wore a home-spun plum colored cotton robe. Around her neck hung many strands of white and orange beads. Her black hair, parted in the middle, streamed loosely down her back to her waist. Her brilliant almond-shaped, obsidian eyes and sensuous mouth gave an exotic touch to her features. Her eyes glittered with an inward flame. She had high cheekbones and her nose was straight for a Maya descendent.

She was short, but not as short as most of the Indian women, maybe five three. Even at fifty years old, her spirit kept her a wild beauty. *Wow! What she must have been like at Chanti's age!* If Chanti's mother had been like her, Jake understood what had attracted her father. Her mother probably had the same vitality, which inspired her to become the risk-taker Chanti said she was.

Jake wished he had known Chanti's mom and dad. They seemed more real to him now. He seldom felt drawn to an adult like he did María. She glided with feline grace toward her granddaughter. Chanti and María hugged. Chanti was a taller edition with the same energy.

As they chattered away in Lacandon, they faced Jake. He heard his name, but understood nothing more. The next thing he knew, María had crossed the space to him and embraced him with great warmth. She stood back, outstretched hands on his arms, and smiled up at him, speaking in words he didn't understand. He did understand the passion in her voice and her happy look.

"I told her you saved my life and she's thanking you."

"Please tell her I was only returning the favor of you rescuing me, more than once."

"She'll have food ready soon. You hungry?"

"What a treat. We won't have to hunt it or cut it down?"

"No. One of Chan Kin's friends brought her an armadillo. It's roasting and there're tortillas."

"Would you please ask her about the satellite phone man?" Jake asked.

Now that I might be able to call, I feel suddenly anxious.

Chanti spoke in rapid Lacandon to her grandmother. María nodded, pointing and speaking more rapid fire than Chanti had.

"He's in the village. He shouldn't be hard to find. We'll look and come back to eat." She spoke again to María and led Jake from the hut.

"Do you have money? He'll probably want some," she asked.

"About 2,000 pesos the last I checked." Jake's heart be faster.

I have so many things I want to tell Mom. I hope she and Chanti will like each other.

"Good. I might be able to convince him without money, but this way everybody'll be happier. He should be in that hut." Chanti pointed to one on the edge of the jungle. "His name's Chan Bor." She stopped and faced Jake.

"Chan Bor comes from a part of the southern Lacandons' territory. There are only about six hundred of us left, half are in the south. There are maybe fifty here in this village. With the deforestation and strangers moving in, the southern Lacandons have pretty much abandoned their traditional way of life. We moved deeper into the jungle to keep our ways as long as possible."

"How've you managed to keep your traditions when no one else did?" Jake asked.

"Our ancestors escaped the fate of all other groups in Mesoamerica, being killed, enslaved or, at least taken in by the Spaniards during their conquest. Most of the southern Lacandons have converted to Christianity and lost a lot of their traditional knowledge. Chan Bor tries to spend time both places so he won't lose everything. He's about my Grandma's age."

"What's Mesoamerica? The same as Latin America?"

"No. It's from central Mexico south, Guatemala, Belize, El Salvador, western Honduras, pacific lowlands of Nicaragua to northwestern Costa Rica. The Spanish Conquistadores never found the Lacandons."

"Okay. Let's go. I hope I can get my mom. She'll be really worried. I should've been in Oaxaca days ago."

They strolled over to Chan Bor's hut. Chanti spoke to the slim man who stood in the entrance. He wore blue jeans, a khaki shirt and huaraches. A holstered pistol hung from his belt on the right side. He had the same heavy lidded eyes of most Lacandons along with the wide mouth. The one thing that set him off from the rest of the Lacandon men in the village was his short western haircut.

"Chanti. Still living in the jungle, I see," Chan Bor said in near perfect English. "Who's this? You're not married are you?"

A red flush spread up Jake's neck into his face.

Chanti chuckled. "No. This is Jake. He's an American who was kidnapped off a bus. He'd like to use your satellite phone to call his mother in the

States to let her know he's okay and figure out how he can get home."

"Okay. Glad to help out. I know how to dial the states, so tell me the number and I'll get it for you."

"One thing, first," Chanti said. "Even though Tenosique may be closer, the rivers are hard to cross. Tell your mom we'll meet her in San Cristobal de las Casas at the Rincón del Arco Hotel, a few blocks from the zócalo. My dad took me there and it's the only place I can remember the name of. It might take us about a week to get there."

Jake repeated the names aloud to be sure he had them.

"I stay at that hotel when I'm in San Cristobal. It's nice," Chan Bor said.

In the jungle, five gunshots cracked. Something large crashed and panted through the thicket. Jake crouched, M14 ready. Chanti had her bow drawn, arrow halfway back. Chan Bor drew his pistol.

Chan Kin lunged through the dense growth and stumbled into the clearing. His chest heaved as he tried to catch his breath. Sweat poured from his face. His eyes widened with fear.

16

Chan Kin sank onto a primitive wooden bench. When he first tried to speak, his voice sputtered. He took a deep breath, lapsed into Maya and kept spewing out words that shot from his mouth so fast Jake couldn't tell where one word started and another ended. Chanti translated a shortened version. He told how he had run into a wild sow with five pigs and barely escaped being mauled to death. He demonstrated how his gun shook when he took aim. He had missed the vicious sow as it charged him. Afterwards, it must have smelled other people because it abandoned the chase before he burst from the jungle. His hand trembled as he fumbled for a cigarette.

Thunderclouds blotted out the sun through the foliage.

"Come in here. It'll rain in a moment." It poured as soon Chan Bor spoke. The huge drops thundered down and threatened to demolish Chan Bor's roof. The phone call would have to wait until the deafening pounding and thunder ended. The lightning cut the black sky with murderous stabs. Crash after crash of thunder shook the ground. A huge double strike of lightning brightened the clearing. Jake jumped at the loudest crack of thunder he had ever heard. The strong smell of ozone flooded Chan Bor's place.

An hour later, the rain stopped as fast as it began. It cooled the air, but when it finished, it grew hot and sultry.

Chan Kin slipped away without saying anything.

"We can try the phone call now," Chan Bor said.

Chanti hugged Jake. "Hope you get her." Jake lost himself in her eyes.

Snapping out of it, Jake repeated the information he needed to tell his mom. Chanti nodded, smiling. Chan Bor dialed the numbers to get out of Mexico and Jake's number and then thrust the phone to Jake.

"Ready to go," he said.

The phone rang nine times. Jake's head drooped. He was ready to disconnect. A click sounded.

"Hello."

His head snapped up, bringing his shoulders erect. A big smile lit his face.

"Mom? Is that you, Mom?"

"Oh, Jake. Jake. Are….are you okay?"

"I'm fine. Don't worry, I'm safe. I love you, Mom."

"I love you, too. Oh, Jake. I've been so worried. I imagined all kinds of bad things happening to you. I'm so glad you're safe. And your Dad's going crazy. He's in Chiapas now. We heard you were kidnapped, but escaped and they were after you. Did they hurt you? "

"No. I got away in a dugout on the river. Boy, do I have some stories to tell you. But they can wait."

"We heard you were last seen running down toward a jungle river with the kidnappers following. Where are you now?"

"I'm still in the middle of the Chiapas jungle. Talking on a satellite phone."

"What happened? You just vanished. You've been gone for days."

He'd never heard his mom sound so anxious before. She was always calm and in control. Even when her favorite mare was down and she tried to save its life.

"They never caught me, thanks to a new friend. Her name's Chanti. I'll tell you all about it when I see you. We're in the middle of the jungle and it'll take a few days for us to get out. Chanti says our best bet is to get to San Cristobal de las Casas."

"Wait. I'd better write it down. Okay."

Jake spelled it and told her about Rincón del Arco, the hotel a few blocks from the zócalo.

"It's the only name Chanti can remember, so we'll meet you there. Better not expect us any sooner than a week from now."

"Your Dad'll be relieved. We'll meet you there. He's in the town of Tenosique. I'll call his hotel right away. How will you get through the jungle? Isn't it dangerous?"

"Chanti knows how. She's great. You won't believe what's happened."

"I'll be on the next plane out of Albuquerque. Are you sure you're okay?"

"Can't wait to see you. I'm fine. Don't worry. I love you, Mom. Want you to meet my friend, Chanti."

"Let me talk to her, Jake."

"Chanti, my mom wants to say hello. Her name's Sharon Brandon."

Chanti took the phone from his outstretched hand.

"Hello, Mrs. Brandon."

"Hello, Chanti. It sounds like you've been taking good care of Jake. I can't thank you enough."

"He's pretty good at taking care of himself."

Jake's face lit up.

"I'm looking forward to meeting you in San Cristobal. Can you get there all right?"

"Yes. But it's hard to tell exactly how long it'll take. It could be less than a week or more. Don't worry. We won't let anything stop us."

"Thanks again. See you soon. Can't wait to meet you. May I speak to Jake once more, please?"

"Jake." Chanti handed him the phone.

"Hi, Mom. I have to go. I don't want to use all Chan Bor's minutes."

"Okay, Jake. I love you. I'm so relieved you're safe. Please be careful getting to San Cristobal."

"Love you, Mom. We'll take care. We won't be able to call again, though. See you soon. No worries. Chanti's fantastic in the jungle. She's lived here all her life."

"Bye, Son."

Jake walked over to Chan Bor to return the phone.

"I have some money. Can I pay you for the call?"

"Won't be necessary. You've had quite an experience. Chanti told me how you saved her life."

"Well, she saved mine more than once."

"Thanks, Chan Bor," Chanti said. "María's waiting to feed us."

"Yes. Thanks very much." Jake shook hands with Chan Bor.

They followed the odor of cooked meat to

María's.

The roasted armadillo and tortillas were mouth-wateringly good. Jake refilled his plate three times. Chanti and María talked, but Jake couldn't follow the conversation and remained silent, stuffing food into his mouth.

After the meal, Chanti stood. María and Jake joined her at the doorway.

"We'll leave in the morning, Jake. María'll have some food for us. We can't take too much 'cause it'll spoil in this heat, but enough for a day, at least."

Chan Kin materialized from the jungle's wall and hurried up to Chanti. He rattled off some Maya. She turned to Jake.

"He says there're four men skulking around near the boats. One of them's a big, heavy man with a mustache. Probably our chiclero friends. They're armed. They've been looking at my boat, so they probably recognize it."

"They might try to steal one. Should we go down there? We need your boat and your friends need theirs," Jake said.

"Yes. When we get close, we'll move off the path and creep down to the river without them seeing us."

As they talked, Chan Kin sat on a bench resting and smoking. He watched and listened to the jungle's sounds.

He grabbed his rifle. Jake flinched.

"Turkey," he whispered.

He aimed toward a treetop two hundred feet up for a second and fired. The turkey plummeted through the leaves and thudded onto a branch forty feet above the ground. Resting his 22 against the tree trunk, Chan Kin shinnied up the tree, unsnarled the bird and threw it to the ground. After sliding down, he picked up the carcass and carried it to María. She accepted it with a smile.

Both armed, Chanti and Jake jogged down the winding trail toward the river. Chan Kin followed. When the path curved to the left before passing the cornfield, Chanti led off to the right into the rain forest at a slower pace.

This feels a lot more comfortable than when I first stepped foot into the jungle.

The three of them slid through the dense growth like ghosts. Jake smiled. They made no more noise than a small creature scurrying along. He checked that the safety of his M14 was off.

They crossed over a ridge above the water's edge in single file, Chanti still leading. Jake stepped on a loose stone. It started an avalanche of clattering pebbles.

Oh, great. Just when I was thinking how good I was getting.

He staggered past Chanti down the sandy hillside, flailing his free arm to maintain his balance. His right hand clutched his rifle in a white knuckled grip. Before he reached the river's whitewater, he dug his heels in and ground to a stop.

A clattering sounded from the jungle in the direction of the docks. Someone had heard them. Someone was coming. Maybe two or three.

There were no voices, only the sound of feet scrambling toward them. *Uh, oh. We can't get captured or killed now. Not after everything we've been through. If we run, they'll be sure to hear and see us. If we stay here, they'll find us. Why am I thinking this way? We're better shots than they are and almost as many as them.* Jake gritted his teeth to fight the hollowness in his chest.

Slipping through the undergrowth, he slid behind some large rocks and crouched, hidden. Chanti and Chan Kin followed, trying to make themselves two feet tall.

Jake listened to the footsteps coming. Twigs snapped. A branch cracked. They picked their way over the ridge without speaking. He gripped his M14 in his wet hands. Sweat dripped from every inch of his body and soaked his hair. The humidity must have been 100%.

He waited, not knowing what he was going to do.

He expected one of the short chicleros to be the first thing he saw. The footsteps sounded only feet away, now.

17

The largest tapir Jake had ever seen pushed through the thick undergrowth and staggered over the ridge. Its 700-pound bulk half slid down on its haunches to the river's bank. It stopped no more than thirty feet from Jake. A long tongue slipped out and slurped at the fast flowing river water.

The tapir froze midlick and lifted its head. It snuffed the air. Finding Jake's scent, it wheeled and stormed away, making enough noise for a marching band.

Phew. I can't believe I was so worried about a tapir. It really sounded like men walking.

Jake slipped into the thick growth along the river's edge to a spot where the docks showed through a small opening. His M14 still gripped in his hands, he scanned the boat area and the riverbank above. Nothing. No Lacandons, no chicleros. Chanti crouched beside him on his right and Chan Kin on his left.

They peered through small windows in the wall of vegetation separating them from the docks. Nothing. Nobody. Only the dugouts tied to the rickety wharf.

"All the boats are still there," Jake said.

"Let's watch for a while," Chanti said.

When the heat became unbearable and the insects drove him to distraction, Jake said, "Enough. Let's move."

They crouched and slipped through the undergrowth into the clearing by the docks.

Kneeling, they scanned in all directions. A couple of Chan Kin's comrades strolled down the path.

After a brief discussion with them, Chanti said, "They haven't seen the chicleros. Let's head back, but keep a sharp eye on the jungle. They'd like nothing better than to get revenge."

They strode up the hill leading away from the water. Jake liked stretching his legs after eating so much, but they slowed their pace once they reached the crest. Jake on one side and Chanti and Chan Kin on the other, they stole along like shadows, eyes darting everywhere. When they reached the village, Jake relaxed.

"Luego, Jake, Chanti," Chan Kin said as he sauntered off toward a group of teenage boys flipping their knives into a tree trunk, 22 again slung barrel down over his shoulder.

"Thanks, Chan Kin," Jake said.

"Let's go to my place. I have a machete for you, although it probably needs to be sharpened. We'll get another hammock down, too." Chanti said.

Both hung from her thatched ceiling. After they hung his hammock and netting, she handed him a whetstone.

Chanti said, "Why don't you sharpen that and then come over to Grandma's. I want to spend some time with her before we leave." She paused and her eyes moistened. "I may never see her again," she whispered.

"Okay. See you soon." *Does that mean she doesn't know if she'll come back? Because of danger or maybe she'll come with me?* Jake thought about Chanti going to New Mexico with him while he worked the stone over the double-edged machete. His pulse quickened. He drew the whetstone faster and harder.

Naw. She just means because of the jungle's danger..... Or does she?

He tested the sharpness against his thumbnail. He didn't know if he could shave with it, but it would do. After cleaning up some with water from a bucket, he strolled over to María's, forcing his trembling legs to work. He inhaled a couple of deep breaths.

Jake gasped at the sight of Chanti. His heart pounded against his chest. This was a softer, warmer woman than he had seen. She wore a loose, blue-colored robe, open at the throat, with a single string of white beads against her golden skin. Her unbraided, tousled hair hung down to her shoulder blades and begged to be touched. She had mischievous, lively eyes Jake could slip into and never find his way out.

He tried not to stare. Chanti saw that and flashed a devilish grin that knocked him back a step.

Grandma María smiled, watching them, and clasped her hands together. Jake couldn't take his eyes from Chanti.

María walked to him and put her arm around his waist from the side. Startled, he looked down and she began her rapid fire Lacandon again. He recognized the same smile as Chanti's. He hugged her.

Chanti gave him a look of such pride he would remember it as long as he lived.

"Grandma seems to think you're attracted to me. And me to you. Is that true, Jake?"

It's so like her to be blunt. What do I say? My face must be scarlet. "I-I think you could safely say I like you more than I've ever liked a girl before."

"Igualmente. We're friends. You're kind and brave. You learn fast and you never quit. I'm really happy I met you."

What does she mean, friends? I was kinda hoping for more. "I'd like it very much if you'd come back to visit my mom and me in New Mexico. Would you?" Grandma María still had her arm around Jake. She hugged him again and chattered to Chanti.

"She wants to know what we're saying," and Chanti explained to her grandmother, who replied without losing her smile.

"She hopes we won't stay away forever, but she thinks it's a good idea to visit my father's land. We'll see. I'd like to, at least for a while. I can't promise anything, but I have papers I'll take with me, dual citizenship with passports from both countries."

At least there's a chance.

The 100-degree weather and overpowering humidity made Jake feel dirty as well as faint from the heat. Every morning his clothes were already wet when he put them on.

"Let's go to the river and get clean and cool off," Jake said.

"Sure. It's too hot. Wait'll I change." Chanti jogged over to her hut.

Jake smiled at María, wishing he could talk to her. She returned his smile and chattered away. *Funny. I don't feel uncomfortable at all. I remember meeting my old girlfriend Ellen's parents last year and how awkward we all were.*

"She says she's glad you came," Chanti said as she came back, wearing her usual outfit, but with her hair still down. "You ready?"

"Okay."

Side by side they headed for the trail leading to the river.

They drew close to the dock area.

"Uh, oh," Jake said.

"Yeah. There's a boat missing," Chanti said. "I don't think anyone from the village left, or I'd know about it."

"Must be the chicleros stole it," Jake said.

"We'll have to be careful tomorrow when we go. The first part of the trip'll be by boat. There's a place I've wanted to explore for a long time where I think there're Maya ruins. I hope that's not where they're headed, but they couldn't know which way we're going."

By this time, they stood together on the embankment a little downriver from the docks. Removing his shoes and laying his weapons beside them, Jake edged into the water, staring hard to detect any snakes or other amphibians. Chanti did the same. Once in up to their shoulders, they took off their clothes to wash.

"Keep moving or the fish will bite your legs," Chanti said as Jake yelped from a nip at his calf.

"You said there're no piranhas, didn't you?" Jake shuffled his feet to scare away the fish.

"Right, but these fish do bite and sometimes painfully."

After rinsing his trousers and shirt well and scrubbing himself, Jake wanted to get out. Another fish bite on his heel made him forget the welcoming coolness of the river. Slipping into his clothes, he climbed out and sat down on the bank. Chanti stayed in the water, unaffected by the fish.

Sitting on grass and moss, Jake relaxed and lay back. As he turned his head to watch Chanti, something moved in his peripheral vision. Locking his eyes on that spot, he discovered a huge, hairy spider two feet from his head. Tarantula. At least six inches across.

I can't win. I've heard that these things get as big as a dinner plate in the Amazon. They even eat birds. At least this one isn't that big.

Jake gasped as the hairy creature gave a hop straight toward his face. It landed inches away as Jake wrenched his head aside. He clenched his stomach muscles and sat up so fast his momentum carried him straight to his feet. He took two quick steps forward and turned. The big spider retreated into the brush.

Chanti chuckled as she stepped from the river. "You moved quicker that time than when the croc went for you," she said. "Don't worry. They're not too aggressive and not nearly as poisonous as many spiders. Now that you had a nap, you ready to go back?"

"Yeah. Long day. It'll be dark soon."

Jake trudged up the trail while Chanti sauntered, smiling the whole way, teeth very white. Jake caught on and his walk changed to match hers. Fatigue no longer bothered him. Shadows showed everywhere. They looked into every potential danger spot. When they arrived at Chanti's place, Jake entered and sat on the old bench by the door.

Chanti said, "I'll be right there," and disappeared.

She returned in minutes with a big leaf filled
with rice and beans. They shared it. It was dark
now. Jake could hardly keep his eyes open. "I'm
sorry. I need sleep,"

"Me, too."

At 4:30 a.m., monkeys in the trees overhead
gave their wake up call, followed at 6:30 by the
toucans, driving away all thoughts of sleep. Jake lay
awake in his hammock.

A cold chill ran down his spine. He
shivered. Something wasn't right. A slight
movement caught his eye below Chanti's hammock.

18

Chanti slid from her hammock and stood.

"Check your shoes, Chanti," Jake said, feeling a strange presence.

Her gaze flashed to the floor. Increased daylight showed color in her running shoe.

"Coral snake," she said. "Thanks." Her machete appeared in her hand, sharp edges gleaming.

Chanti kicked over her shoe. As the snake slithered onto the floor, the machete streaked toward it. The headless body squirmed on the floor, spurting blood.

"I'm beginning to really dislike snakes," Jake said.

"There're snakes everywhere. They crawl over the roof and then come into the hut. They drop on the floor, or onto the nets over the hammocks," Chanti said.

Chanti slid her machete under the snake's body and with one smooth motion, lifted it and flung it outside. The head followed. She grabbed a bucket of water and sluiced down the floor.

"How'd you know?"

"I don't know. I had a strange feeling something was wrong."

While she cleaned, Jake struggled from his hammock and checked his shoes. When he knocked the second one's heel against the floor, a large scorpion popped out. His shoe rose and fell, crunching the scorpion into a wet spot.

"Did I mention I hate scorpions, too." Jake used his machete to flip the remains outside.

"Not a good start to the day, but better than being bitten," Chanti said. "I'll be right back. I'm going to Grandma's to get breakfast."

When she returned, Jake had packed all his things for the trip in a small backpack Chanti had given him. She carried a big leaf filled with rice and beans.

"Last night we ate rice and beans, but this morning it's beans and rice," Chanti said. Despite joking, she remained strangely silent while they ate.

After they finished, Chanti said, "These hammocks, the netting and plastic tarp to cover them all, role up tight and fit in the backpacks."

She rolled hers tightly and stuffed the bundle into her pack. Jake followed her example.

Looking around the room, she said, "Let's say goodbye to Grandma María and get started. We'll pick up some food, too. Some of that turkey." Chanti's voice was so low, Jake strained to hear it. Her head slumped. She looked deflated.

Jake didn't know what to say so he kept quiet. This was the first time he'd seen her sad. Even after near death with the chicleros and the puma, she had thrived on the situation and seemed indestructible.

He let her lead the way to her grandma's. María stood in the doorway and smiled when she saw them. Stepping down in front of Chanti, they embraced and held each other for a long time. Several tears leaked from Chanti's eyes. Jake stopped next to them and when they broke apart, María hugged him.

Chanti disappeared into the hut and came out with two bulging sacks. Jake stuffed his into the pack and slung it over his back. Picking up his M14, he waited while the two women spoke in Maya. Chanti kissed her grandmother's cheek, turned and strode toward the path leading to the river. Jake followed after a quick wave to María.

Many villagers paused to watch and wave. Chan Bor stood with a group of Lacandon men talking. He left them and approached.

"Safe journey. Hope to see you two again."

"Igualmente." Jake stepped forward and shook his hand.

"Take care, Chan Bor. Thanks again for the use of your phone," Chanti said. "I don't like goodbyes," she said to Jake as they continued down the trail.

Chan Kin and his group of teenagers waited at the docks.

"You give big gun, now, Jake?"

"I need it till we get out of the jungle. Those chicleros're still around."

Chan Kin and Chanti spoke in Maya for a moment.

"Thanks for your help, Chan Kin. I'll try to get the rifle to you," Jake said.

Chanti glanced at Jake and untied the bow rope from the dock. They boarded the canoe one at a time, a hand on each side of the boat. Jake sat in the stern and, waving once, they shoved off into the river.

Jake experienced a mixture of feelings. Sadness to leave new friends he might never see again and excitement to be off on a new adventure with Chanti. At the moment, these overpowered the need to see his mom.

That makes me feel guilty, but not much. She knows I'm okay, now. I might never come this way again.

"I wish I could see Ba lam before we go," Jake said.

"Me too. He'll be okay if he doesn't try to find us and stays in his own territory. I got him started in that direction. We've been together a long time. I'll miss him."

Does that mean she doesn't plan on returning? She's going to New Mexico? Naw, it couldn't be. But maybe she'll visit for a while.

Neither Jake nor Chanti paddled hard cruising downriver, letting the current do most of the work. In a short time they arrived at the junction with the big river and turned with the flow.

The dense jungle thinned and a scattering of huts appeared. A lone woman walked between two of the structures on bare feet. She was another replica of the ancient Maya, the same cheekbones, forehead, eyes and long black hair.

The shoreline rose at least five feet above the water level. There was no dock, but some steps had been cut into the bank and a dugout rested above. They stopped paddling, but Jake used his oar as a rudder.

When they passed the tiny village, they looked up a narrow inlet created by a clear stream through the two-hundred foot mahogany trees. A small Indian girl bent low to fill a gourd with stream water. Her colorful, flowered dress made it easy to spot her.

A large boa burst from the water.

The child screamed and dodged away from the black maw when it struck at her.

The snake shot out of the stream.

It wrapped its heavy coils around the shrieking girl and dragged her toward the water.

Jake and Chanti dug their paddles into the river, surging toward the stream. They turned into the cove. Powerful strokes ate up the yards separating them from the struggle. They beached their canoe on the low bank almost on top of the snake.

Unable to use his rifle because of the girl, Jake drew his machete and leaped ashore beside Chanti.

The snake rolled and pulled the helpless child under the water. Her screams ended in a series of bubbles.

Without thinking, Jake dove in after her. He spotted the snake's writhing coils.

A small arm and leg protruded. The hand seemed to wave at him.

Chanti swam to the squirming mass. She reached out to the small hand. Small fingers gripped hers. The girl lived. Chanti plunged her machete into the thick coil. The huge snake rolled away, jerking the small hand from Chanti's grip.

Jake found himself staring into the coldest eyes he'd ever seen. The open mouth struck at him.

He ducked aside and thrust his machete at its throat.

He missed and the big snake's jaws fastened onto his left forearm like a vice.

He struck again with his machete.

This time, his aim was true. The fine-edged blade slid into the throat and severed the spinal column.

The big boa rolled in the water, twisting Jake with its teeth still fastened to his arm. Jake hacked at its throat trying to chop off its head.

Chanti found the little girl's hand and tugged her free. Surfacing, she held the sputtering girl up to the air and climbed to dry ground.

Jake finished hacking through the snake's neck and broke the surface of the stream, gulping air. He tugged the ugly head off his gashed forearm and hurled it into the jungle.

"Aargh," he shouted. "Did I mention that I hate snakes."

While climbing out, he slipped and fell to his chest on the slick bank, then scrambled the rest of the way up.

"She okay?"

"She's frightened to death, but she's breathing. She'll be fine."

Chanti held the fragile child to her chest and talked to her in Maya, rubbing her back. The girl stopped sobbing and her breathing slowed while her arms encircled Chanti's neck.

The woman they had seen from the boat scurried over. Up close, deep wrinkles lined her aged face.

She must be the grandmother. She looks much older than María.

Chanti and the old woman spoke for a while as Chanti handed her the child.

"She's thanking us and wants us to come up for food, but I told her we need to continue our journey, that we have a long way to go. You ready?"

The small girl clung to her grandmother. Tears gushed from both their eyes.

"Yes," Jake said, swallowing hard. "Let's go."

Chanti said their goodbyes to the pair and they both waved. Tears trickled down Chanti's cheeks. They climbed back into their dugout. Chanti reached into her pack and brought out the salve she kept for injuries. Jake rubbed it into the punctures on his forearm. The two of them shoved off into the stream. He brought them about and they headed back into the river.

"Shouldn't we tie our packs to the boat?" Jake said.

"Let's do it, now, while it's calm."

They finished tying their packs to the cross pieces

"You were great," Chanti said. "You didn't stop to think, which is sometimes the best thing. Not always, but she wouldn't have lasted long."

Jake's heart swelled in his chest. "We took care of the one that attacked Ba lam, so I figured we'd be okay. I might have hesitated if I'd been alone."

"I doubt it. You're brave. You do what needs to be done. I'm glad we're together."

Together how? What's she mean. I should just ask her. Maybe later.

Chanti said, "I thought I was satisfied being alone - before you came into the jungle - but I don't know if I want to go back to that life. I'll miss Ba lam, but change is good."

"Are you going back with me to New Mexico?"

19

"I've thought about it. Maybe. What worries me is, I've been alone so long, maybe I wouldn't fit in. I'm not used to doing anything someone else wants me to do," Chanti said.

They launched the canoe into the river and guided it to midstream, Chanti in the bow and Jake in the stern.

"We get along fine. No worries. Mom believes in letting people be who they are."

"Since Mom and Dad died, I've come and gone whenever and wherever I wanted. I'd hate to put us both in a bad spot. We'll talk some more."

"We live on a ranch. Lot's of space. You wouldn't feel closed in. Mom doesn't give me too many rules to live by. The best thing to do, would be for you to visit and find out for yourself. You don't have to make up your mind beforehand."

"Maybe so. I've never had a close friend outside my family. Until now. I don't know much about that. It scares me."

That's strange. She wasn't scared when she had a knife to her throat or when she faced the puma. I guess I don't understand females.

The boat sprang back from a bone shaking collision. Jake's chin snapped down to his chest. Chanti tumbled into the dugout's bow on her knees.

An equally startled crocodile plunged downward into deep waters. Two seconds later the monster vanished without a trace.

"Sorry. Too busy talking," Chanti said.

She's so full of confidence in most things and so honest, she doesn't worry about saving face if she makes a mistake, and she doesn't make a big thing of it, either. She's so different from the girls back home.

The wind picked up. Bumpy rapids stretched across the river's width. The boat bounced over them. White water sprayed Chanti's clothes and drenched Jake. The current accelerated and plunged them into the churning chasm.

Their boat's speed increased.

The trees along the shore became a blur.

The thundering roar grew louder. The river dropped many feet in a few hundred yards creating a tangle of massive waves and roiling currents.

The powerful flow forced them into a narrow rock-filled gorge that twisted back and forth. Rocks were so hidden in the spraying foam, it was next to impossible to see them. Jake and Chanti concentrated on paddling, pushing off from rocks, leaning into turns and hanging on. Anything to avoid a collision at full tilt.

The rugged dugout ricocheted from one rock to another. It never collided head on with a boulder, but glanced off with the help of paddles pushing it away. The river threw the boat above a huge, sharp-pointed rock. The violent wave tossed Chanti forward onto the bow rail. She righted herself, thrust her oar down onto the boulder and pushed. Jake fought to turn the small boat in the same direction. As the boat dropped out from under them, it glanced off the rock's side.

Chanti needed every bit of strength and agility she possessed to stay in the vessel. It hit the frothing water and lurched away from the rock. Jake dropped his oar to the boat's deck and grabbed onto the sides to remain upright. The heaving boat veered to the left. The swerve forced him to lean far out over the side. The dugout careened back under him and dumped him on the deck.

They found no time to rest. Another boulder appeared. And another.

Running the rapids was like going down a river-sized pinball machine, except that rocks don't go "ding" when they're hit.

The crazy trip lasted two minutes, but felt like hours. They floated in calmer water, bodies slumped, heads down, gasping for breath. The riverbanks widened. The flat walls that reached up a thousand feet above the tumbling water of the rapids grew shorter. The jungle closed in again.

"Check for leaks. I'll bail the water," Chanti said.

"Whoever built this did a great job," Jake said, patting the canoe's side. "Not a leak, but we've taken on some water."

Chanti began bailing with an empty gourd tied in the boat's bottom. She passed it back to Jake who finished the job.

"This rapids was tougher than the one I went through by myself."

"By the way, I built this boat," Chanti said. "This isn't one of the large rapids. If it were, we'd have to get out and tow it. There's a cataract coming soon we'll have to portage around. It'll be tough carrying this dugout."

The river propelled them around a bend. An explosion of cannons rumbled. Jake had never heard a noise like that.

"Cataract," Chanti said. "Pull for shore. That way." She pointed to the right. They beached the dugout.

"We'll tow the dugout because the current's very strong here. Near the waterfall, there's a place we can use to portage around it. I came this way a few years ago with my dad. It might be hard to find, 'cause it'll be overgrown," Chanti said.

She led the way, clearing a path along the shoreline with her machete. Jake followed, towing the boat with the bowline. Every hundred yards, they switched jobs in the midst of sprays of water sparkling in the midday sun. Sweat poured down their backs and chests. Their hair looked like they had been swimming.

"Let's rest, now. We're going to cut through there." Chanti pointed downhill, shouting to be heard over the thunderous waterfall.

They washed in the river, drank water and ate turkey with rice and beans. Jake collapsed against the boat's bow and fell asleep. He awoke to Chanti shaking his shoulder.

"We need to get started. This'll probably take the rest of the day. Let's pull the dugout up on shore and hide it. We'll have to make two trips. First, we'll cut a path and carry our packs and gear. Next, we'll come back and carry the boat. It's heavy. We'll trade off cutting and carrying like we just did."

"I'm ready," Jake said, but his shoulders sagged. He drank as much as he could hold. Chanti did, too. She seemed as indestructible as always. They had already filled their canteens after boiling the water over a small fire. Covering the canoe with branches, they brushed out all traces of their footsteps from the shoreline.

They spent the afternoon hacking a half-mile path around the falls. Every hundred yards or so, they changed jobs. One slashed the dense jungle undergrowth and the other carried both packs together with weapons and canteens.

Jake couldn't remember ever being so hot and tired. He had worked hard on their ranch, but this was like working in a steam room all day.

The roar of the cataract stayed with them every second. Mist sprayed up from the pounding waterfall. When Jake and Chanti arrived at a site below the falls, they flopped in the grass, nearly unconscious.

Jake drained his canteen and struggled to a spring's edge to refill it. He filled Chanti's, too.

"It's getting late. Let's get this over with," Jake said.

They brought their canteens and machetes with them. The rest of their gear remained hidden in the brush near the fall's base.

"The sooner the better. We can rest afterwards. Wanna race back up?" Chanti's eyebrow lifted. Her lips curled into a smile.

"No. You're very funny," Jake said, poking her in the arm.

She put one foot in front of the other and trudged up as slow as Jake. Halfway, Jake's thighs wanted to crumple. His legs trembled.

"Chanti, stop."

"You okay?"

"I need a drink and rest." *That's amazing. It doesn't bother me anymore to say that to her.*

Jake again finished off his water. Chanti, also. "I needed that, too," she said.

Five minutes later, Jake rose on steadier legs. "I can make it, now."

I have that something extra. I feel great. Nothing can stop me. Almost there.

Once they reached the dugout and uncovered it, they drank as much as they could. Shouldering the boat, Jake leading, they set off down the rough trail. He remembered in times like this, when his body was worn out, accidents happen. He fixed his gaze on the path so he wouldn't twist an ankle. At the halfway point, they took a ten-minute break. Both slumped against a tree trunk, heads hanging.

Afterwards, they finished the agony and staggered to the bottom. *Phew. I'm tired.* They set the canoe on the river's bank

"I can't believe we did it," Jake said. He flopped against the boat and let out a whoosh of air.

Chanti smiled. "You did great. I don't know anyone else who could have done it."

Jake's tiredness fled. His chest swelled. His chin lifted.

I can't lose her. If she doesn't come to New Mexico, I might have to stay here.

He strode to the river and threw himself on the bank to drink. When he finished, his stomach felt so swollen, he had a hard time getting up.

"I hate to bring this up, now, but we better move down river. This big pool under the falls attracts lots of animals at night, including jaguars."

"Well, let's get it over with," Jake said. "Once I lie down, I'm never getting up again."

Together, they shoved the canoe into the water and tied the bowline to a tree branch. Each struggled to pick up their gear and secure it in the boat. Untying the bowline after boarding, they dipped their paddles in and shoved off. Jake was content to use his as a rudder and the dugout floated along a few feet from the shoreline.

A thick, rope-like body stretched along an overhanging branch. Half of it hung down toward the water. Jake guided the boat out toward the river's center. The large boa pulled itself up and slithered out to the limb's end. It watched Jake and Jake watched it.

"There," Chanti said, pointing to a beach area.

Jake steered the canoe straight for the shore. Hopping out, they pulled the boat onto the stony beach. Dragging their gear up the bank, they selected three trees where they could hang their hammocks. They ate in the growing darkness and climbed into bed, too tired to speak.

Jake awoke in the dark, groggy. *Where are we? Oh, yeah. Below the falls.*

The full moon's glare reflected from the water. What woke him up?

A jaguar's coughing grunt came from the jungle fringes. Were they being hunted? Soaked in sweat, he fumbled for his M14.

20

In the moon's sparkling glow from the river, a spotted shadow glided along the perimeter of the clearing.

Jake held his breath.

His finger rested on his rifle's trigger.

Another coughing grunt. The tawny cat crouched at the water's edge to drink.

Wheeling, the jaguar charged downriver along the bank. Jake gasped.

"You nervous, Jake?" Chanti whispered.

"Just a little."

"Go back to sleep. Still a couple hours till daybreak."

When Jake awoke at first light, it surprised him he'd fallen back asleep. His mosquito netting sagged, leaving a two-inch space over his chest. A long shape squirmed on the netting.

Jake's machete lay at his side and he grasped the handle. Using the flat of the blade, he flipped the heavy snake away. It flopped against a rock on the edge of the rain forest. He slipped from his hammock.

Not again. Barba Amarilla. I'd better kill it.

The five-foot viper slithered from their camp into the thick rain forest growth. Jake let it go, not wanting to follow it into a trap.

"Good choice, Jake. They're too dangerous and strike like lightning." Chanti crawled from her hammock. "You amaze me. You learn fast."

Jake's morning sluggishness fled. He stood straight and grinned.

Chanti pointed to a shaggy palm along the shoreline. "Coroso. Good to eat. I don't know what it's called in English. Bring your machete."

Together they hacked through twenty-five hard scales on the trunk from opposite sides and chopped until the tree crashed to the jungle floor. Chanti cut and yanked out a foot and a half of firm white substance.

"Raw, this tastes like nuts. Cooked, like chicken. We need a fire." She lifted the Coroso heart and stood. "Watch out for that tree," she said as Jake put his hand on the fallen trunk to push himself up.

A large, hairy tarantula ran from under the bark. Jake jerked his hand away and jumped back. He squashed the spider into pulp with his shoe.

"I should've warned you about that. They like to hide there."

"Let's skip the fire and eat it raw," Jake said.

"Sure. No sense spending the extra time to cook." She hacked it into strips and they squatted between their hammocks to eat. They looked into each other's eyes and Jake felt lost, like he could never find his way out, and didn't want to.

Afterwards, they walked to the water's edge. Scanning everywhere first for danger on land and in the water, they washed. Compared to the air, the water felt cool. Chanti produced her red bug repellant salve and they smeared it on.

"Not too far ahead, there's a hilly place where I think the jungle hides an ancient Maya village. You seemed interested in the ruins where we met the chicleros. You still interested in exploring? We won't spend too much time. If you don't want to go, I'll understand."

"Sounds good. I may never come this way again."

"I might not, myself," Chanti said. "I've only been here once before."

"Let's load up the boat."

After packing and tying down their gear in the dugout, Jake pulled and Chanti pushed the boat into the water. Chanti's bow and arrows and Jake's M14 lay in the boat's bottom. Chanti glanced back to their empty camp.

"Jake," she said.

The tone of her voice caused Jake to follow her look.

"Oh, no," Jake whispered.

Three dwarf-like chicleros stood at the clearing's border. They looked much the same as before, unshaven, clad in huaraches, and filthy white trousers and shirts. Perhaps they were even dirtier now.

Jake smelled them.

All held rifles aimed at the two of them.

"Pigs," Chanti spat.

The large, fat boss man, still wearing rundown boots, sweat soaked khakis and safari hat, stumbled from the jungle. His clothes looked like he had been swimming. His lips drew back in a grimace exposing rotten teeth.

He swaggered toward the canoe. The three followed. Jake gagged from the stench of their unwashed bodies. One of the short chicleros stepped up beside the boss. Both stopped directly in front of Jake. The big, mustachioed boss was uglier than Jake remembered. A long, ridged scar ran down through his clouded left eye and his droopy mustache to the corner of his mouth. His good eye was a dark pit.

The three rifles no longer pointed toward Jake and Chanti. Their enemies seemed to think they controlled the situation, believing the two feared them.

The big one spoke rapidly in Spanish. Chanti translated.

"He says he's been waiting to get us alone. He's going to kill us."

The sweat-soaked fat man reached across his body and drew his revolver from his left hip.

Jake blocked the draw with his left hand gripping the pistol.

With Ba lam's speed, his right hand flew to the man's throat, rigid fingers driving into it.

His left hand tore the gun from the man's hand and streaked across to smash the smaller man in the temple. Both dropped like stones. The action lasted three seconds.

Chanti stepped forward and kicked the closest of the other two in the testicles. He doubled over.

She snatched his weapon and slammed the butt into the fourth man's head.

Chanti rotated and smashed the doubled over one the same way with the rifle butt.

Jake finished off the boss man by ramming the pistol butt into his skull.

He took several deep breaths to calm down.

Funny how my body reacts afterwards. My legs are shaking, but they didn't before.

Chanti hugged Jake. Flabbergasted, he hugged her back.

And she makes them just as weak.

"Incredible. I never saw anyone react faster than that," she said, looking into his eyes.

"You were just as fast," Jake said, face growing red. "When he said he was going to kill us, I didn't think I had any choice. If we were smart, I guess we'd kill them now. Otherwise we may live to regret it. But I can't do that in cold blood. They all seem to be breathing."

"I agree. We'll just have to pay more attention. If they shot first, we'd be dead. They probably wanted to enjoy our fear. It would make them feel macho. Let's make it tough on them and tie them up. There's some rope in the dugout."

"I'll get it."

Together they trussed up the unconscious chicleros and boss on their stomachs, feet together, drawn up to their hands behind their backs. They held their breaths as long as they could, but needed to take several. Both retched each time they sucked in a breath.

"Maybe that Fer de Lance or the jaguar will come back and save us more trouble," Chanti said.

Jake stripped the holster and shell belt from the fat man. He carried the three rifles and pistol to their boat and set them in the bottom. He slipped the belt around his waist and dropped the revolver into the holster on his right side.

"Hey. I feel like a cowboy, now."

"You need a big hat."

I feel really good. I can't believe I did that. I came close to not trying it. Sometimes it's best not to think, just act. If I'd taken time to think, it would've been too late.

"Don't look, now, but the canoe's gone," Jake said.

They both sprinted to the river's bank. The dugout had drifted down river ten yards and about four feet out. Jake chopped a path along the dense shoreline until he was even with the boat. Searching for predators first, he waded out and grabbed the stern, pulling it back to shore. Chanti pulled the bow in so it floated parallel to the bank.

"We have everything. Let's go," Chanti said.

They boarded and launched themselves downriver. The river narrowed and they cruised along in the middle, letting the current do most of the work. They rounded a bend.

On the far shore, a well-muscled puma crouched on a boulder. The big cat's unblinking stare was intimidating. The tawny color and the white underbelly and muzzle of the 225 -pound cat glistened in the sunlight.

The huge cat, eyes never leaving them, leaped fifteen feet straight toward the boat onto another rock on the edge of the torrent. Jake looked through his M14's sights right into its cold, amber eyes. The lion had black tipped, rounded ears.

"I think he's even bigger than the one Ba lam killed," Jake said.

As they drifted past, the lion remained on the boulder looking at Jake and Chanti for what seemed an eternity, its long, dark tipped tail twitching side to side. Jake held his breath.

What a beautiful animal. He must be starving to risk coming this close to man. His eyes haven't left us for a second. Apparently, he never needs to blink.

As the canoe swept down river, the puma turned back toward the other side, still watching them over his shoulder. For a short ways, he swam and then waded the remaining distance to dry land. He padded off through the trees and didn't look back.

"I'm glad we didn't have to kill him, he's such a magnificent creature," Jake said.

"Yes. This is his territory and we're the invaders. But we might meet again."

What does she mean by that?

Chanti stowed her bow back at the bottom of the boat. Her arrows stayed in her quiver slung across her back.

The boat had drifted dangerously close to the lion's side of the river and Jake steered back to the middle. A half-mile further, wide and fast flowing, the river curved to the right. Thick, green vegetation lined its misty banks.

"There, Jake," Chanti pointed to a beach of stones. The jungle receded for twenty feet. It was clear the high water mark was several yards above its current level.

Scary. Imagine what the rapids would be like. It's hard to picture so much water.

Jake guided the dugout into the stone-littered shore. The two of them pulled the boat up the steep bank into the tree line. Removing their gear and weapons, they covered the dugout with branches and erased their footsteps and the drag signs from the boat.

"Is this where you think the ruins are?" Jake asked.

"About a half-mile in. Thanks for agreeing to explore."

"Wouldn't miss it."

With their machetes working full time, they hacked a trail into the rain forest. Jake and Chanti left the fringe growth alone so their entrance would be invisible from the river. A few feet in, both followed a dirt path made by animals seeking water. They passed through a dense bamboo grove. Beyond grew thick clusters of ferns that rose to Jake's shoulders.

Chanti, in the lead, held up her hand and stopped.

A snort?

They listened.

Nothing.

Is my imagination playing tricks on me? Or am I just getting jumpy?

Then the rustle of soft padding footsteps, coming closer.

21

Jake and Chanti crept up to a sun drenched clearing in the pathway.

A chill ran down Jake's back.

A perfect place for a trap.

They stopped, huddled next to lush green ferns. Before they left the rain forest's canopy, Jake froze for a few moments in knee high grass, listening.

He shivered. His finger curled around his rifle's trigger.

Chanti had an arrow in her bow, half drawn.

Both weapons pointed toward the open space and the thick vegetation on the clearing's far side.

Amid the ferns, glared two unwavering amber eyes.

The big cat stood motionless, partially hidden in the fronds inside the tree line.

The eyes watched them coldly.

He crouched so close, Jake could count his whiskers.

He's hunting us. I only saw his eyes because some light glinted off them. Too bad. Now I know it'll be him or us.

Jake's M14 sighted straight for the puma's chest. He didn't fire. He watched and waited.

The mountain lion snarled and leapt toward them. An arrow struck its upper chest at the height of its leap.

At the same time Jake's M14 fired a bullet into the chest a little lower. Jake shot again, but the puma was already dead. He plunged to the floor of the clearing five feet in front of them.

"What a waste. At least this time we were prepared and didn't need Ba lam to save us," Chanti said.

"Yeah. Good thing. Sometimes I hate that everything's hunting everything else. But then I think of the good things. You, Ba lam, María and the beauty of this place and I feel great again."

"Reload and let's go," Chanti said. She removed her arrow from the dead cat's chest with a Herculean tug, tearing it out.

"I hope my ammo lasts 'till we get to San Cristobal," Jake said. *Hope Mom's okay. I feel guilty not going straight there, but I never felt this way about a girl before. Mom'll understand. I hope.*

In the short time they had been in the clearing, cumulus clouds darkened the sky and it grew cool with spotty bursts of rain. The showers created a mist that rose up from the ground to waist level.

Chanti took the lead. Streams flowed on either side of their chosen path. She led them across a slippery tree trunk bridge. Jake picked his way across above sharp rocks resting in the streambed. He didn't want to break a bone.

The howler monkeys provided a constant roar from the trees on every side.

Sounds like something out of a horror movie.

They threaded their way through the dripping rain forest, past a sleeping butterfly with a wingspan the size of a man's hand. A huge moth as big as a small bird fluttered by. Blue and white markings covered its brown wings. Every few minutes a strange bird cried out, sounding like a whistle blown under water.

"We're close, now. A few minutes more," Chanti said.

The sun peeked through a space in the clouds. A toucan perched three yards from them on a tree branch. The bright yellow beak flashed like a signal light as it flew off, crossing an arm's length in front of their eyes.

Nearby, visible through an opening in the trees, water cascaded down a cliff into a pool big enough for swimming, maybe 30 by 50 feet.

"Let's cool off and wash," Jake said.

"Good idea."

Chanti hacked her way toward a clearing around the pool. On the fringe, She paused. Jake stopped beside her.

"I see it," he whispered, standing motionless.

An animal swam toward them, a fish in its mouth. Dark spots and stripes showed on its head between rounded ears. The cat waded from the water and shook itself, sending a shower spray all around.

"Ocelot," Chanti whispered in Jake's ear. "They rarely hunt in the daytime."

The ocelot's fur was a dark yellow blending into brown covered with darker brown, uneven shaped spots and stripes edged with black. A lithe, medium sized cat, its slender body stood maybe four feet long and weighed no more than thirty pounds. It ate the fish in large gulps. Raising its head, it sniffed and bounded off into the jungle.

"They're probably the prettiest cats I've ever seen," Chanti said.

"I thought they were smaller than that," Jake said.

"That's a big ocelot. I'm glad you got a chance to see one." She reached out to touch Jake's arm. "There aren't many left. They're hunted for their fur and trapped for the pet trade. Not many people see them in the wild."

"I never saw a big cat catch a fish before."

"They're good swimmers. They also eat small deer, rabbits, rodents and reptiles."

Laying their weapons beside the pool's bank, they peeled off their clothes and waded in. The shallow water of the pool's edge, created a perfect place to sit and wash. Jake no longer felt any embarrassment about their nudity, although he tried not to stare. They rinsed their clothes first, tossed them on the grassy bank, plunged in and swam to the falls to stand beneath the cascading water. The change in temperature covered his skin with goose bumps.

Wow. This feels fantastic. I hate to get out.

"The place I think might be Maya ruins is just a short distance. Ready to go?" Chanti said, as she leaned on Jake's shoulder so he heard her under the thunderous falls, causing more goose bumps.

"No. But I will."

They waded to their clothes and gear. The clothes, under the scorching sun, should have been almost dry, but the humidity kept them damp. Dressing in damp clothes was nothing new.

Chanti led and used her machete to clear a trail. Brighter light showed ahead.

She stopped on the edge of a grassland, covered with low bushes and heavily spotted by trees. The grass grew waist high and vines covered many of the trees. Where they stood, mahogany trees rose to majestic heights. The hanging roots of a banyan tree flowed down beside them. Further out in the open, Spanish moss on tall trees rippled in the breeze.

Strange-shaped mounds covered with dense vegetation rose from the grass. Some were sheer-sided. A few trees sprouted from the mounds' tops while bushes grew from the sides.

"This is it," Chanti said.

"Not as dense as we just passed through," Jake said.

Near them, beyond the tallest hill jutting up, stood a green lagoon, perhaps as wide as a football field across. On the far bank was an entrance hole to a cave, half submerged in the water. It arched up above the lagoon, big enough to drive a car through. Only ten yards along the bank, another entrance opened up.

"We'll have to explore those caves," Jake said, pointing.

"Wait'll we get really hot. Look at this big hill. I think it's a pyramid. It looks rounded off, but for hundreds of years the jungle has taken over, covered everything and filled in the crevices and cracks."

"Yeah. I saw a Catholic church built on top of a large tree-covered hill, which turned out to be a pyramid. It's in Cholula in the state of Puebla and is the largest pyramid in the world. I was on a trip with my dad. It looked funny when the lower part of the pyramid was exposed, hard to believe. It was a lot bigger than the church, but only ever partially excavated. The interior passages are open, though."

"This one's pretty high. It sticks up over the treetops. Let's take a look. I'll go around the base this way and you go that way. Look for a spot where there's not much dirt covering the stone. Maybe we can find an entrance. We'll have to probe with our machetes."

They started together then peeled off in opposite directions. Jake used his machete to test the depth of the soil on the pyramid's sides. The hill's base spread out far enough so examining it would take a while. Jake stuck to his task and covered one side in a half hour. The soil layer was too thick. Sweat dripped down his forehead into his eyes. His clothes stuck to his skin like they were glued. No shade. A bright furnace in the sky.

Chanti called out. "Jake. I've found a place where there might be a doorway."

Happy to abandon his job, Jake jogged around the hill. Chanti dug into the earth with her machete. Her arms and legs glistened with sweat in the sunlight.

Jake joined in, using his machete as a combination digging bar and shovel. Chanti had uncovered one side of a stone-arched portal and Jake worked on the other side. Once exposed, the archway was no larger than a double door on a modern house. A couple hours flew by. Inside, dirt had piled up in a mound over the centuries, extending several feet back into the entrance. Their chests heaved. They slumped to the ground.

"Break time," Chanti said. "I don't think we need to waste hours clearing that pile out. We can climb over it."

"We'll have to sharpen these machetes later. Mine's pretty dull."

Both drank from their canteens until empty.

"I'll fill these up in that spring we passed on the way here, if you want to make some torches," Jake said.

"We passed several of the trees to get sap from back there. Let's go."

They separated upon entering the rain forest. Jake threaded his way through the thick undergrowth to the spring. He filled the canteens and slashed his way back to the tree line. The machete did not slice through the brush easily, sometimes glancing off.

Chanti appeared without a sound several minutes later.

She still moves like a ghost. I'm tuned into the jungle, now, yet she constantly amazes me.

"Ready to explore?" She asked.

"Yep. An extra torch, eh." Jake said, referring to the fact she carried three instead of two.

When they reached the opening, Chanti lit two of the torches, handing one to Jake. He slung the M14 across his back, barrel down, but they left their packs inside the doorway.

Jake clambered over the dirt mound and Chanti followed. A tunnel stretched before them, constructed of rough stone blocks. Unused for hundreds of years, it smelled musty and damp, rotten, and the temperature dropped a full ten degrees.

Jake bent over slightly as he edged along the rock littered tunnel, built for short Mayas. His torchlight flickered, throwing moving shadows everywhere. He half expected to see a Maya warrior step out from the murk.

The torchlight's short reach pushed back the darkness for only a few feet before the dense gloom enveloped it. They inched along, protected from the frightening blackness by the tiny umbrella of light.

A high step showed in the torch's glow. As Jake stepped forward, the bottom of a narrow stairway appeared, leading up. They climbed, counting fifty high steps, so narrow they had to scramble up sideways because their feet didn't fit straight on the steps. At the stair's top, a flat expanse awaited them. Close by, within the sphere of torchlight, stood a stone statue of a reclining figure with a flat stomach.

Jake moved a few steps into the Stygian gloom.

The light bubble moved, too.

Two eyes glittered from a stocky black jaguar.

"Uh, oh." Jake whispered.

22

Jake drew his pistol like an old-time gunfighter. The gun came up in a blur.

He didn't fire. The black cat stood immobile in the shadows.

Chanti dodged to his side. Somehow, she had an arrow drawn and aimed.

Jake stepped forward with his torch held high in his left hand. The umbrella of light lit up the animal.

"It's not real. Only a statue," he said. "Wow. Kind of a shock seeing that here. Made my heart jump start."

"Look how smooth it is." Chanti stepped up to the jaguar and ran her hand over the statue's surface. "And it's kept its color all these years. That other flat figure was used to make sacrifices and offerings on."

"What're its eyes made of?" Jake said.

"Jade or jadeite, I think."

Holding his torch high with the scare over, Jake said, "The walls here are smooth, too. Look at the paintings."

"And the ceiling's covered with them," Chanti said.

"I feel a breeze. There must be an opening."

"Over in that corner. See the tree roots coming down?"

"Yeah. There's a pile of debris under them," Jake said.

"Look at this painting of a huge head," Chanti said. She ran her hand along the wall to the right of the entrance.

The painting still kept much of its color after centuries of being enclosed in the tomb. The head showed the typical Maya broad face, high cheekbones and long, slightly curved nose. A large, red and yellow-colored feathered headdress fitted on his head. The figure gripped some type of bowl. He wore gold bracelets and necklaces.

Jake joined her and they slid across the corner to a continuation of the colorful murals on the next wall. For more than an hour Chanti and Jake examined the four walls and ceiling. The paintings showed in detail the royal court rituals, including human sacrifice, costumes, musical instruments; trumpets, drums, flutes and rattles; and weapons of war; clubs, spears, knives. Some scenes were faded, but a surprising number held their red, blue, white and yellow colors and details.

On the ceiling, an extra vivid scene depicted two types of birds flying over a building that might be a cage. A lot of red and yellow birds on a white background.

"Amazing. I'm glad we came," Jake said.

"Thanks. I know you want to see your mom soon." Chanti hugged Jake from the side. "I always thought this place might be hidden ruins since I came here with my dad. We didn't have time to explore then and I planned to come again."

"I almost feel disloyal to Mom, but I wanted to come. Besides, you saved my life and this is the least I can do. This's great. We have old Indian sites up in New Mexico, too. I like visiting them and exploring. Lots of petroglyphs and pictographs, like here."

"Let's go down the other stairway for a quick look. Our torches are about finished, but we'll use the extra."

As she spoke, hers sputtered out. She lit the extra from Jake's, which was much dimmer, now. Chanti led the way to the opposite stairs. As they started down, Jake's torch burned out.

The stairs descended about twenty steps and the tunnel turned left. The air grew cooler, but stale. Continuing ten yards down the curving passage, Chanti paused. A sound above. The ceiling was higher. A colony of bats clung to it, hissing and squirming as Chanti lifted the torch.

"I might have to add them to my list of snakes, scorpions and spiders," Jake said. "They're ugly."

"Nothing to worry about."

About five more yards, they discovered a small room with what looked like a stone bed. The room appeared otherwise bare. They passed two more identical rooms.

"Maybe we'd better turn back. Before this torch burns out," Chanti said.

"It wouldn't be fun traveling these steps in pitch darkness."

Descending the steep, narrow steps proved more difficult than going up. And scarier.

"I remember going down steps like these on the big sun pyramid at Teotihuacán outside Mexico City. A woman was sitting on the steps part way down and I asked if I could help her. She said she couldn't go another inch, it was so scary, and just sat there. But I went back a couple weeks later and she was gone," Jake said, smiling.

"I've heard of that place. I'd love to go there."

They reached the bottom, picked up their gear by the portal and crawled over the mountain of earth blocking it.

"I think we deserve a rest after all that," Chanti said. "Let's head over to the lagoon."

"Won't get any argument from me."

"Watch for snakes."

They stepped nimbly through the tall grass, eyes glued on the ground, searching for an enemy. When they arrived at the lagoon's bank, they checked the water for predators. Chanti led and followed the shoreline around to the far side. They stopped on the bank's top while directly over the first cave.

"This flat rock is a good place to leave our stuff. We're gonna have to swim into the cave," Chanti said.

Jake cleaned some grass and brush away from the steep bank's edge. "We're in luck. Old steps cut into the bank. I'll clear them of brush to make sure there're no snakes, scorpions or any of my other favorites before I take my shoes off."

"Good idea."

A few minutes and he cleared the small, worn stairway cut into the stone. Jake had parted the brush along the side with his machete to check for snakes, too.

They covered their gear and weapons on the flat rock with the brush Jake cut from the steps. Nothing would glisten in the sunlight and give away their position. Jake kept his sheath knife strapped to his waist and Chanti kept her machete. Easing down the rounded, slippery stairway, they slipped into the water and swam into the cave.

The second cave, ten yards further, was another entrance to the same underground chamber.

Enough light poured through the two openings to make a torch unnecessary. A narrow ledge ran along the far wall, rising a foot above the water level.

"Look at those rock carvings," Jake said, pointing toward the back wall. "Let's get up on the ledge so we can see better."

They boosted themselves from the water onto the green-slimed ledge and examined the petroglyphs. The one in front of Jake seemed to be two dancers.

"They look a lot like carvings of dancers I've seen in pictures from Egypt," he said.

After admiring it for a few moments, Jake stepped over to the next one on the left and Chanti slid over to the right.

Jake said, "Here're two warriors with typical Maya faces and noses wearing fancy headdresses and ornamental robes, or maybe some kind of armor. They carry war clubs, too."

"This one's strange," Chanti said. "A big skull with a snake coming out of its mouth instead of a tongue. I think there's some type of bird sitting on it, too. Hard to tell."

"Here's one that seems to be a lot of geometrical figures. No idea what they represent. Almost looks like a maze," Jake said.

Chanti stood at her next one. "I think this might be the Maya god Kukulkán. They built the famous temple at Chichén Itzá in his honor. The Aztecs called him Quetzalcoatl. Shows a warrior or priest with a spear. He has a huge feathered headdress like a serpent's head with a wide-open mouth. Inside the mouth you can see the man's face."

"This last one looks like a human sacrifice just took place. I guess the standing man is a priest. He's holding a knife in one hand and a dripping heart above his head in the other. A man is lying on an altar like the one we just saw in the pyramid next to the jaguar. It looks like a hole in his chest where they ripped the heart out," Jake said. "Looking at these is incredible, but I'm so hungry I feel weak. How about you?"

"I thought you'd never ask. We'll find food, set up a camp and come back later or tomorrow. I think we'd better make some torches, too, to explore here. There may be a passage back along this ledge."

Diving back into the water, they swam out of the cave and clambered up to their gear. Retrieving their weapons and packs, they tramped off toward the pyramid, pausing at the excavated entrance.

Chanti said, "Let's leave our packs here, inside again. When we get back, we can set up our hammocks in these trees. We don't want to be close to the lagoon because of all the animals that come there at night to drink, including jaguars and pumas."

They hiked back into the jungle the way they had traveled from the river. After cutting through the brush with dull machetes, they took a break beside a stream.

As they sat on a log, something fell from a tree. Chanti and Jake looked up. Two wild turkeys perched twenty feet above them, pecking at their feathers.

Jake aimed his rifle, but an arrow thudded into the nearest turkey. The other bird squawked and flew deeper into the rain forest, hitting the foliage with flapping wings. The dead turkey flopped to the forest's floor, glancing off several branches on the way.

"That's one of the fattest turkeys I've seen," Chanti said.

"You picked the right one. We oughta get a couple of meals from it." Jake tore the arrow from the bird and handed it to Chanti.

"Over there is some guiro. Remember, it has black meat that tastes like cantaloupe. I'll get some, and we need torches, too."

Jake picked up the dead bird by its feet, while Chanti slipped through the undergrowth to get the guiro.

"Feast time," Chanti said as she rejoined Jake and dumped the guiro at his feet. "I'll make four torches, two each."

She vanished as she merged into the underbrush and returned a short while later with huge-knobbed torches that would last longer than the previous three.

Jake carried the turkey in one hand and the guiro loaded against his stomach, held in place with his forearms. "Need a shopping bag," he said.

Chanti led with the four torches over one shoulder and her machete in the other hand.

In single file they worked their way to the grasslands.

They paused on the forest's fringe. A loud crack sounded, perhaps a dry branch. Galloping hooves snapping off smaller branches followed.

The thudding grew closer.

23

Jake and Chanti dropped their torches, turkey and guiro.

Jake pointed his M14 toward the hoof beats. Chanti stepped alongside Jake and drew her arrow back, ready.

A grunting sound accompanied the pounding feet.

Then silence.

Two beady dark eyes mounted on a mound of bristly black hair, peeked through the undergrowth.

Enormous, yellowed tusks thrust up from the black boar's lower jaw. It woofed and retreated.

A second creature, possibly its mate, took its place, grunting and growling. A sow. Three piglets stuck close to her, two black and one brown. Dark stripes ran down the backs of all three.

Chanti and Jake stayed put, motionless, not wanting to provoke a charge by the snorting animals.

The sow squealed and snorted and stalked menacingly back and forth. The young pigs watched.

She wheeled and lunged into the forest, back the way they had come. The young ones charged after her. The big boar had already disappeared. Soon, their grunting and footsteps died to silence.

"I hoped we wouldn't have to kill any. We have enough meat. But when one charges you, there's no choice," Chanti said.

Picking up their food, they continued to their cache. Jake built a fire pit while Chanti cleaned the turkey she shot a short time earlier and cut up the meat. They spitted and roasted it. A mouth-watering feast. After devouring turkey and guiro, Jake wanted to sleep. First, he had to set up his hammock. Darkness would come soon. Chanti did likewise.

"That was great turkey," Jake said.

"Sure was. Sometimes there's plenty of meat and other times it's scarce. If we'd had to, we could have got some at the lagoon tonight, but that might be dangerous."

They sat side-by-side watching the sun set. Jake's hand stole over to Chanti's and held it. She squeezed his and didn't try to withdraw hers. Jake relaxed as a comfortable feeling spread through him.

I know I'm only fifteen, but I could stay with her forever. She makes me feel good and she has every quality I admire. Is this love? Wonder how she feels?

Later, when the fire died out, she leaned over and kissed him on the cheek, rose and said, "I need my sleep, but we'd better sharpen our machetes, first."

"Okay. We're going back to that cave tomorrow, right?"

"First thing after breakfast."

Maybe she does love me. Naw. She's probably treating me like a friend. Should I ask her? Tomorrow if I feel brave. Funny. It's easier to face danger than ask a simple question.

After honing their machetes to razor sharpness, they crawled into their hammocks. Jake was drifting off when a bird barked at the moon like a hound dog, over and over. The jungle echoed with the roar of howler monkeys. Hunting jaguars and pumas disturbed their peace. The mosquitoes and bugs became a nightmare, buzzing, but unable to penetrate their netting.

Jake smiled to himself and fell fast asleep anyway.

Chanti climbed from her hammock early and started a fire. The cool air blew across the lagoon, causing Jake to shiver as he stretched. After slathering on the red bug repellant, they squatted by the fire as they ate guiro and a slab of turkey. Plenty remained for their evening meal.

"I guess we'd better take these hammocks down and hide everything," Jake said.

"Let's cover up this entryway, too. No sense advertising."

They heaped brush over the piles of earth and the doorway to the pyramid. It wouldn't fool a close inspection, but would camouflage it from a distance. They stowed their packs inside and carried their weapons and two torches each. When they reached the flat rock above the cave entrance, they hid Jake's M14, newly acquired pistol and Chanti's bow and arrows under brush at the rock's edge by the steps. Jake left his shirt there, too.

Descending the steps, they slid into the cool, green water and swam through the entrance to the cave, holding the torches above water. Climbing from the water onto the ledge, they looked around.

"Let's follow this ledge to the right," Chanti said. She lit one torch and led the way.

They edged along the slimy ledge for perhaps twenty yards. The cavern's ceiling sloped lower and lower.

"Look," Chanti said. "The underground river comes from there."

The roof met the water. Blocked. With a second look, it seemed to leave an opening of a couple of inches above the water's surface. Chanti held the torch near it.

"I think we can get through here," she said. "You're a better swimmer than I am. Want to try first?"

"Sure. I'll take a torch and light it on the other side. If there's any place to go to."

Jake slipped into the water and Chanti handed him a torch and her lighter. He swam forward into the narrow passage. His hand slid along the scummy surface of the wall, pitted with ruts, cracks and small holes. He ducked his head under the low spot. The roof continued to slant down.

He shivered, not because of the cold and damp, but the irrational fear of the unknown; swimming into the water-filled tunnel where his breath might run out before getting air. He grinned and commanded his fears to go.

He breathed in and out several times, holding his face up to the small air space next to the ceiling. Jake took a deep final breath and dove forward. He swam for fifteen or twenty seconds when the ceiling angled sharply up. Reaching up with his hand, he felt the angle of the ceiling rise above the water level. Swimming a few feet further, his head broke out of the water. He let out a sigh of relief and drew a deep breath.

The air smelled musty. He held up Chanti's butane lighter and flicked it a couple of times before it caught. The flame flared and threw weird shadows on the rough walls. A dark, water-filled tunnel disappeared in the darkness beyond.

Putting the lighter back in his pocket, he submerged and swam back to Chanti. She held her torch from her position on the ledge, Statue-of-Liberty-like.

He called out, "Chanti. We have to swim under water for a short distance. You can make it. Come on in. You can hold onto my belt if you want."

"I'll be okay." She eased herself into the water. "New experience for me. Go ahead. I'll follow. Don't go too fast, though."

"Wait till the roof gets down to the water before we go under." Jake set off with a slow sidestroke, keeping an eye on Chanti. When they could go no further on top of the water, he paused," You ready?"

"Let's go."

"Take some deep breaths first and then a final one," Jake said. He slid under the water and disappeared. Knowing exactly how far it was made it easier. It seemed shorter. When he came up, he didn't need a deep breath.

She's brave. She's a poor swimmer and she's going into an unknown most people would find terrifying. I'm a good swimmer and it scared me. She must trust me, like I do her. Mom'll like her a lot.

While he waited, treading water, he pulled the torch from the back of his belt and lit it. He held the lighter's flame to the torch longer than usual. An unlit corridor with the river flowing through it led to a dark opening. Chanti popped up beside him and grasped his shoulder.

"That would have been really scary if I'd had to do it alone, or go first. I doubt if I could have. It was bad enough as it was. You're very brave."

"Looks like a bigger room ahead," he said. "Come on." Jake tugged her hand.

Sidestroking and holding the torches above water, it took only moments to get to the corridor's end. Chanti wasn't a natural in the water. Jake glided through while she splashed and struggled to keep up.

The huge cavern gobbled up the torchlight. A shaft of light shone through a ceiling hole high above the pool of water that spread out from the narrow corridor. Vegetation grew around the hole and down into the chamber, blocking a lot of the light.

"Let's swim over to the side," Chanti said, gasping, working hard treading water. Jake floated easily.

They swam to a wide ledge along the cavern's wall and pulled themselves up onto the slippery edge to rest and catch their breath. The air was thick and musty. The cavern's ceiling slanted down to meet the wall and low hanging blood red limestone stalactites oozed from the dripping roof.

Their eyes adjusted to the light level and a bizarre world took shape. Spaced between several stalactites hanging over the green pool, dangled the roots of trees that had penetrated the ceiling in their search for water. They dropped 50 feet to the pool's surface. Along the ledge, several stalactites met stalagmites, forming continuous columns.

"This looks like an upside down underground forest," Jake said.

"Over on the other side, it looks like there's a rocky beach, but I can't see past it."

"Should we swim over?"

Chanti slid into the water and Jake followed. Reaching the other side, they waded out on the gradually rising floor of stones. Not far down the cobbled pathway, another shaft of light reflected off the water's surface, illuminating the cavernous room's sides. The stalactites and stalagmites thinned out there.

Passages branched off from the huge chamber. Through a large opening, twice as tall as Jake, they discovered another room. In its center stood a rectangular stone altar. On one end rested a stone bowl.

"That bowl might be what they drank the sacrificial blood from," Chanti said.

"The air seems fresher here. Maybe another entrance?" Jake said.

"I feel the fresh air, too."

Chanti walked to the far wall where a doorway they hadn't noticed opened up.

"Look, Jake."

Cooled by a flow of fresh air from the opening, they followed the draft, which grew stronger as they crept along a well-beaten path through a large, winding tunnel. The bubble of light from their torch didn't extend far enough for them to walk fast. Anxious to explore, they passed by wall paintings. A ledge ran along the corridor about four feet off the floor. Every so often a doorway, the size of a window, appeared over the ledge.

"Those must lead into a cave or some kind of a room," Chanti said.

"Let's take a quick look," Jake said and vaulted onto the ledge. He stuck his torch into an opening followed by his head. "Lots of pottery. Uh, oh. Skeletons, too. We'll check them out later."

"I smell smoke," Chanti said.

Jake dropped down from the ledge. Chanti continued in the same direction.

"Put out your torch, Jake. It'll be safer with only one for a while."

Does she sense something? She's pretty uncanny that way.

As they rounded a curve in the tunnel, a light stronger than theirs glowed further down. Chanti doused her light.

Flattening themselves against the tunnel wall, they watched a short man wearing the standard Mexican *campesino* outfit of baggy pants, cotton shirt and sandals. Unlike the Lacondans, he was filthy.

"Chiclero," Chanti whispered. "Smell him?"

He held a bright camp light of some kind in one hand and a rifle in the other. He shuffled toward them.

A second one appeared behind him. And a third.

Their circle of light approached, too close now.

24

Jake and Chanti moved together, retreating as if they were one.

They slipped along the wall back the way they came.

The *campesinos* trudged on, drawing nearer.

The two of them paused at the passageway's curve, looking back. Jake half expected to see the big, beefy mustachioed thief in the soiled khakis who wanted to kill them.

Instead, a slim man of medium height with combed dark hair strolled with feline grace behind the other three. His long, narrow face flashed bright white teeth in taut olive skin. He wore an immaculate white shirt, pressed khakis and shined boots. A pistol hung from his waist in a polished leather holster. It reminded Jake that all he and Chanti had was a knife and machete.

"I've seen him in Tenosique," Chanti whispered. "He deals in stolen antiquities, but on a much bigger scale than the others we ran into. Very dangerous. A bigger crew than they had, too. It's rumored he kills people who get in his way."

They backpedaled around the tunnel's curve. Far down that section of passage, another light bubble loomed. Four distant figures shuffled along in their direction. All had rifles.

"We seem to be in trouble," Jake whispered.

"Let's see if we can get into that cave up on the ledge," Chanti said. "Run."

Chanti and Jake flew through the tunnel, bare feet weightless, hardly touching the passage's floor. They sprinted on their toes. No flapping feet to reveal their escape. Almost no sound. Chanti got there first and vaulted onto the ledge. Jake trailed a second behind. Chanti eased into the dark, yawning hole. Once past the tiny crawl space, she flicked on her lighter.

The chamber's walls extended out of the weak illumination's range on both sides of the doorway and to the rear. She edged to the side and Jake slid in beside her. On the left lay dozens of human skeletons, heads against the wall. On the right, rows of pots and pottery.

Jake looked into the space on either side of the doorway. He touched her shoulder and pointed. They crawled to either side, flanking it. Jake squashed a black, long-legged spider on the floor with his knife. Chanti waved her machete through thick cobwebs. Squatting, flattening their backs against the wall, Chanti put her lighter out. They waited, easing their breath in and out.

Light glared from both directions in the tunnel. The chicleros called to each other. A strong glow flashed into their hiding place, illuminating the ceiling.

Jake looked across at Chanti. She had her machete up and ready.

He clutched his own knife in a sweaty hand, held at waist level.

From the ledge whispered a rustling noise. A blinding light flowed through the portal. Someone's brown hand stuck a lantern into the chamber. A dark Maya face followed, along with a strong smell of sweat.

Jake held his breath, blinking against the sudden radiance, knife poised.

The chiclero stared straight ahead. If he looked either way, he was dead. Chanti's gleaming, razor-like blade hung over his neck.

A voice from outside the tomb spoke. The head inside grunted in response and withdrew, pulling the lantern after it.

Jake let out his breath.

Chanti had held hers, too.

The light in the tunnel thinned out to a faint glow.

Chanti stuck her face half way out and looked toward the lantern.

"They're looking in another room like this," she said. She watched. Soon, the glimmer disappeared.

"They've gone out of sight. We're safe for the moment. Trouble is, they're in the direction we need to go to get back." She ignited her torch. The brilliance illuminated a large pot beside her. "Look at this." She showed him a painted scene of three trumpeters, brown trumpets aimed into the air, standing in front of a priest or king seated on a throne. "This place is a treasure of Maya antiquities. I think those men are exploring right now. They'll start stealing artifacts soon."

"We need to go back the way we came. We might get out of here from the direction they came, but I don't want to go through the jungle barefoot."

"That's the shortest way back to our weapons. Let's try the tunnel, the way we came. If we see lanterns, we'll hightail it back here," Chanti said.

"I'll go first in the dark and you follow with a lit torch. That way the light's range won't show when I get to the next curve, but it'll help me get through the passageway."

They dropped down to the tunnel floor and Jake set off in a fast stride. Chanti waited to give him a head start, then shadowed him, keeping pace. When he reached the curve in the wall, he halted. Chanti stopped at the same distance from him. He poked his head around the bend.

"Nothing," he said.

"Let's keep going. We'll make a run for it if we have to. I know I'm faster than they are and you're probably faster than me."

I doubt that. She just beat me to the ledge. Maybe in a longer race.

They stole down the tunnel to the smaller chamber of the stone altar. Jake peeked into the room.

"Looks okay."

While Jake checked out the gigantic chamber through the doorway, Chanti looked closer at the smaller room.

"Look at all the paintings of sacrifices."

'We probably oughta get out of here while we can," Jake said.

"How's it look?"

"I see torches off to the right. We can go left, which is where we came from, anyhow."

Chanti snuffed out her torch and they paused for a moment to allow their eyes to get accustomed to the semidarkness. Jake led the way onto the stony beach.

Another lantern loomed in the direction they were headed. Surrounded again. Caught out in the open, Jake and Chanti searched for a secure place.

"There," she pointed to an opening in the wall, hidden behind a stalagmite. They stumbled across the rocky section to the black hole.

"Ouch. Tough on bare feet."

Chanti tiptoed into the murky entryway, took a couple steps further without being able to see and lit her lighter. Another passage led back into the rock. It curved to the right and when they passed the bend, she set fire to her torch. Similar to the last tunnel, its ceiling was low, created for shorter Mayas. Both had to duck and walk awkwardly.

They plodded to a shaft leading upward. Chanti pointed to the worn steps in the wet, slippery rock leading straight up.

"What do you think? Want to go up? We might find an exit close to where we came in."

"Might's well," Jake said. "Let's put these torches through our belts in back. Leave our hands free. But you go first and I'll stay below with a torch lit so you can see. Then, when you're at the top, you light yours so I can."

The worn stairs, only about three inches deep and sculpted for slightly built Mayas, offered little room for her gringo fingers and toes. Chanti used all her muscle and skill. Jake, larger, had an even tougher time. He counted thirty steps.

At the top of the shaft, another low tunnel awaited them. They squeezed around heaps of broken rock, but halted where a section of fallen stones blocked their way.

"It'll take a long time to pull all this rock away. It might go on for a long ways. We're gonna have to go back," Jake said.

"Maybe the chicleros have cleared out by now."

"Hope so."

"Going down will be much worse than coming up," Chanti said.

"At least it'll be too dark to see very far. It's best never to look down, anyway. I'll go first. You led coming up."

Jake backed up to the edge of the precipice and lowered himself until his right foot ferreted out the first tiny step. He transferred all his weight to that foot. His left foot searched for another step. Clutching the top of the ledge with both hands, he eased himself down. Soon he let go of the ledge with one hand to grip a narrow step. And then another with the other hand. He breathed a sigh of relief and moved down again.

His right foot slipped off its stair. "Ahhh!"

His left followed. "Nooo!"

He clung to two worn, smooth uneven steps with his fingers holding all his weight.

His heart thundered against his chest.

"Jake, you okay?"

"Maybe. Know in a minute."

Jake's right foot struggled to find a hold. The ball of his foot fit on a step and he settled his weight on it. His toes gripped the damp stone. His left foot found one, too. Hugging the wall, he tried to relax one hand at a time without pitching backwards into the abyss. At the same time one hand was free, he wiped its sweaty palm on his pants.

"Okay. I'm on my way again."

He sweated and struggled to the bottom with no further mishaps, but the trip down lasted probably three or four times as long as the climb up. He fired up his torch. Chanti reached the bottom some time later, having started after he was safe at the base. If she slipped, she wouldn't fall on him.

"You scared me back there. I thought you might have fallen," she said.

"It's hard to believe we made it up and back. I might have to add climbing in the dark to my list of snakes, scorpions and spiders."

"Let's find out if we can get out of here the way we came."

Chanti showed the way toward the main chamber. She doused her torch before they reached the opening. Lanterns glared a little to the right. Six men stood around the slim boss, listening to him.

She slipped out the entryway and edged along to the left. Jake followed, clenching his knife in his right hand and an unlit torch in the other. He stubbed his toe on a big rock.

"Ouch!"

Chanti paused, looked at Jake and back to the men's gathering. They still surrounded their boss. Not one took an interest in anything else. Jake stopped beside her.

Come to think of it, what happened to the eighth man? I'm sure there were four in each group originally.

Chanti pointed toward the water with her machete. They would swim from there.

A dark form emerged from the blackness beyond.

Jake gasped and crouched.

The phantom stopped two meters away from them. The eighth man.

His rifle jerked up to chest level, pointed straight at Chanti.

25

In one smooth underhand lob, Jake's knife flew to the man's chest. Thunk. Whoosh. The air left his lungs. Inches away, Chanti's machete pierced the man's throat. A spurt of blood erupted. The rifle clattered to the stones. The dark form sank to its knees and flopped forward to the stones.

Just when I thought we were home free. I can't believe we just killed someone else.

Chanti and Jake took two steps to the fallen chiclero, rolled him onto his back and ripped out their sharp-edged weapons.

The group's conversation turned into shouts. Seven men raced toward them.

A few steps and Jake slipped into the water. Chanti followed. Jake and Chanti slid under the pool's surface and swam underwater. A shot rang out, deafening in the cavern. Jake stayed suspended underwater waiting for Chanti. When her outstretched hand touched his, he grasped it tightly. An electrical sensation ran through him. He quivered all over.

Kicking hard, he pulled her at an angle toward the opposite ledge. He wanted to get out of the line of fire.

She gripped hard to let him know she needed air. They surfaced ten feet from the outcrop. A controlled breath and they ducked under, continuing along the ledge toward the place they first entered the cavern. Jake placed Chanti's hand on the back of his belt so they wouldn't lose track of each other in the pitch-blackness.

When they broke the surface for another breath, they were well out of the halo of light. Jake side stroked along the damp wall, keeping a hand on it to find his way through the darkness. They came to the low ceiling where they would have to swim underwater. Treading water for a few moments, they sucked in deep breaths.

It's scary not seeing anything in the dark for such a long time. Hope this is where I think it is. If not, we might be in trouble. I don't think those men could possibly see us here. Oh, well. Here goes.

Jake submerged. Chanti trailed behind, still holding his belt. The small doubt Jake had about not being in the right place made the short journey take forever.

As he wondered if they would ever get there, his hand broke the surface. Kicking hard, he popped his head up and pulled Chanti with him.

Gasping, she threw her arms around his neck and kissed him full on the mouth. A warm feeling mushroomed through him, but ended quickly as he inhaled water when they sank beneath the surface, again.

"I don't know if I could have done that by myself," she said, while they treaded water.

"Let's get up on that ledge. You still have your lighter?"

"Yeah." She flicked it a couple of times until it lit, so they had a clear picture of the ledge. After boosting themselves onto the stone shelf, exhausted and drained, they sat for a while, side by side. Jake held her hand. She gripped his and put her head on his shoulder.

I could stay here like this forever. Jake wanted to say, "I love you." Instead, he said, "We should probably get started." *Maybe she feels like I do. There're things I'd like to say to her, but I don't know how. I don't want to sound like a goof.*

"I don't want to go, but we'd better get to our weapons and a safe place," Chanti said.

They stood and walked to the opening, where they dove in and swam outside. Climbing the worn stairs, they retrieved Jake's guns and Chanti's bow and arrows. Jake donned his shirt and shoes while Chanti put on her running shoes.

"I don't like abandoning this site to those thieves, but I guess we don't have any choice. There're too many of them. Besides, the chicleros are just fall guys for their boss. They'll get hurt and he probably won't. Maybe as soon as we get to civilization, we can let the authorities know," Chanti said.

"Reminds me of the kidnappers who abducted me from the bus. But their leader didn't turn out to be such a bad guy, like this one."

"Well, let's get back to our packs and head for the boat."

Retracing their path to the lagoon, they arrived at the hidden pyramid to reclaim their packs and food.

"Let's eat now in case we have to run and don't have time later," Chanti said.

After laying everything within easy reach, they squatted by the burial shrine's entrance and ate more of their turkey and guiro.

"We'll have to hunt again tomorrow," Jake said. "We can stop at that spring and fill up these canteens."

"Jake, this is the first time I've felt really safe with anyone outside my immediate family. I trust you to do the right thing. Your reactions are quicker than mine, now. It's nice to be able to rely on you."

"Thanks. But you're still quicker," Jake chuckled and Chanti joined him. "Will you come to New Mexico with me?"

I'm sure not good at being subtle. Oh, well. She's as direct as anyone I've ever met. She can appreciate that.

"I want to, but I don't know yet," Chanti said. "I like you a lot. And not because you're quicker than me. You're a fine, decent person."

"Your Grandma María was right. You owe it to yourself to see your dad's native land."

A rifle cracked in the distance. The bullet slammed into the dirt pile. A geyser of dirt spouted.

Jake and Chanti spun toward the sound.

On top of the flat rock over the lagoon's cave entrance, stood the six chicleros and their slim boss.

Shrugging on their packs and grabbing their weapons, they lunged away from the dirt pile.

A second shot sounded. Followed by another.

The teens bolted around the hill's edge and sprinted flat out for the jungle where they had originally come from. Once past the overgrown pyramid, in view of the thieves again, they zigzagged, slow then fast.

Three more shots cracked. Too far away for accuracy.

They lurched through the fringe of brush and jungle to vanish from sight. Dodging behind two trees, they paused to catch their breath and watch.

The six chicleros raced toward the jungle, bypassing the pyramid-hill. Their boss trailed behind, no longer spotless, but dirty and sweating like the rest.

"Head to the spring for water. Then straight to the boat," Chanti said. She led and Jake cast frequent glances over his shoulder.

Arriving at the spring, they spent seconds filling their canteens. Off again, they slashed through the jungle and dodged around brush, when possible. Chanti possessed a built-in compass. She and Jake trotted across the fallen-log bridge. The dead puma no longer lay in the clearing, a tasty dinner for another predator. Sweat poured off them, as they reached the dugout hidden under the brush-pile.

Stripping the boat clear, Jake and Chanti dragged it to the river's edge and shoved it in. Both tied down their packs and canteens, but kept their weapons ready.

Snatching up their paddles, Chanti jumped into the bow while Jake shoved the canoe further into the water. He boosted himself from waist-deep water over the edge into the stern as the current took over. Together, bending low, they stroked hard to escape the area before trouble arrived.

Jake looked over his shoulder. "I can't believe it. Look who's coming along the river bank."

"I thought we were done with them," Chanti said. The four they overpowered and left tied up before visiting the pyramid site, slogged along far up the river. They never showed a sign they saw Jake and Chanti, too busy straining to get through the thick undergrowth.

After widening the distance between themselves and their launch into the water, they took a breather, coasting with the current.

"Not too far from here, we're going to turn upriver into a smaller waterway. We can stay with the dugout for a distance, but we'll be going upstream the whole way. We can get almost to the town of Chanal. We'll leave our boat at the river's edge and cut through the jungle to get to the village. From Chanal, we can follow the road straight west to San Cristobal."

"We'll be there in no time," Jake said.

"It won't be easy against the current. Good thing is, the river branches keep getting smaller and the flow's not so strong."

They paddled in the river's middle to avoid snakes on tree limbs hanging over the water. About a half hour passed until they came to a smaller river emptying into the big one. Chanti pointed and Jake used his paddle as a rudder to turn the dugout into it. Pausing at the river's mouth, they rested and drank from their canteens.

"Here we go. Keep it slow and steady," Chanti said.

Exhausted, they turned into the bank when the light began to fail. Saw-toothed rock cliffs stuck up along the water's border. A slope from the water to the high bank allowed them to drag the dugout from the river.

"Not much of a place to camp, but it doesn't look any better further on," Chanti said.

"It'll do. I'm beat," Jake said.

"Thanks for getting me through that mess in the cave. I thought we could avoid those men, but there was nothing we could do but what we did at the end. I never would have made it through the water without you," Chanti said.

"You're welcome. You give me courage. Glad I helped."

They built a tiny fire, boiled water to purify it and refill their canteens and wolfed down the remainder of their turkey. Not much, but it would have to do. The few small trees between the cliff and the river supported their hammocks.

"Hey, look at this," Jake said, revived by the food and water. Pointing to a small opening in the rocky wall, he dropped to his knees and peered inside. "Let's take a peek. Make sure there's nothing in there that'll come out after dark."

Jake crawled in and Chanti followed. The cave expanded inside enough so Chanti crept up beside Jake, although they couldn't stand. They waited for their eyes to become accustomed to the semi darkness.

"Might be some jungle beast in here. Smells gamy. Maybe this is a stupid idea," Jake whispered. He stretched out his hand as he started to crawl forward.

His fingers touched a soft, furry ball and he jerked his hand back as if it had touched fire.

A growl echoed through the stillness of the cave.

A snarl followed.

And a rasping hiss.

Jake let out a hoarse cry and fumbled for his machete. He stopped before he drew it from its sheath and chuckled. Chanti, kneeling beside him, laughed.

Three baby jaguars, helpless kittens, growled their defiance. Each was heavily marked with black spots, but not the black rings adults have.

"They don't like us in their den. Aren't they brave?" Chanti said. She put out her hand and they growled again, spitting at her. Chanti laughed and drew one toward her, stroking and roughing it up gently. "Look how ferocious it is."

Jake played with one of the others. It growled and chewed on his hand. "Ouch."

"I think it's time to go," Chanti said. "The mother jaguar would not go far or stay away long. She wouldn't leave these guys to starve."

A sudden urgency to flee overwhelmed Jake, but they had to back out.

No room to turn around.

What if she came back now. We wouldn't have a chance.

26

Jake scooted back on his knees. Two baby jaguars sniffed and snarled at his hands. The third bared its teeth and nipped Chanti's hands as she followed Jake.

Moments later, Jake cleared the cave's mouth and wheeled, alert for danger. Nothing.

Chanti spun to face out. The jaguar kittens stayed inside their den. One sat on his haunches with his ears laid back and growled a few more times before he quieted.

"Jake, we need to get out of here. I don't want to have to harm any jaguar, let alone a mother with three dependant kittens. We'll have to move our camp."

"Let's get started, then. It's almost dark."

They sweated while they took down the hammocks, put out the fire and stowed everything in the dugout.

As they shoved off into the river, something on shore uttered a low, guttural grunt. They looked back as they dug deep with their paddles. A flash of yellow and black ducked into the cave.

"Phew. In the nick of time," Jake said.

They ferreted out a wider expanse to camp in with more trees. Darkness settled over them before they hung the hammocks.

Daybreak came too soon. During the previous day, they had struggled against the current and their backs and shoulders still ached. Jake's palm throbbed from a blister.

They broke camp, lashed down their gear in the canoe and coated themselves with red insect repellant.

Chanti stood straight and tall while she studied the area surrounding them.

"There's some guapinol. It's brown outside and has brown seeds, but inside it's yellow and sweet. I'll get enough for now and later."

She merged into the trees while Jake inspected the lashings to be sure they were fast. Back in no time, she slipped into camp soundlessly.

"Guapinol and mangos, too. Have some."

They ate their fill and stashed the rest in the boat's bottom.

"That's the best mango I ever had. I don't have any comparison for the guapinol. Not bad, though," Jake said.

Paddling upriver soon loosened their stiff muscles. They fell into a rhythm that ate up the miles. An hour or so after setting out, Jake steered the dugout into another smaller waterway at Chanti's direction. The rainforest grew as thick as ever along the tributary. With the sun high at midday, they pulled into shore to rest and eat.

First, they built a small fire to boil the river water in Chanti's battered old metal pot. While they waited, they feasted on the rest of the mangos and guapinol.

Jake dosed off leaning against a tree. He awoke with a start when something thumped into the tree trunk.

Shoving himself forward, he spun toward the tree. His machete flashed up in a smooth draw from its scabbard.

Chanti's machete had pierced a six-foot long brown tree snake with saddle-shaped markings. The snake writhed in pain just above where Jake's head had been, squirming violently on the impaling blade.

Jake stepped forward and ended its predicament by beheading it.

"Thanks, Chanti. I should know better than to fall asleep like that." He ripped her machete from the tree and handed it to her.

"S'okay. As long as one of us is awake. Came close to not seeing it, though. I was almost asleep, too."

"Is it poisonous?"

"Yeah, but its venom usually won't kill you. Best not to be too weak from poison, though."

"How much further today?"

"There's one more river to go up. Don't know exactly how long it'll take. It's called the Rio Tzaconejá. We'll follow it up to a couple miles from the town of Chanal I told you about. Cutting through the jungle, it won't take too long to get to the road to San Cristobal."

"You ready? My mom's probably anxious to see me safe."

"Okay."

The afternoon passed with the monotony of paddling. When Jake thought he might lose his mind from the humidity and heat, they entered the last turn. He guided the dugout into the river. Continuing upriver, they found a flat spot to camp on the shore. A grassy shelf protruded five feet above the water level.

Jake eased the boat into a parallel position with the shore. Above them loomed an immense yellow mangrove with its huge root system jutting from the water higher than a man. Chanti tied the boat's bowline securely to a root. After they disembarked and unloaded their weapons and gear, she tied the stern line to another root.

Overhead, a spider monkey with black hands dangled from a branch. Her small baby clung to her neck, hanging down her back. The baby's huge eyes peered over its mother's shoulder at the two of them.

After setting up camp and lighting a tiny fire, Jake and Chanti sat back to back. They rested against each other and kept an eye out for danger.

"We're in the land of the Zapatistas now," Chanti said. "Even if we run into any, we shouldn't have trouble. My dad knew some. They're good people for the most part."

Jake said, "My dad told me the Indians here are poor and the Zapatistas have been fighting to get them more rights."

"Yeah. It's a never-ending cycle. Children rarely get beyond primary school. They have little chance to break out. My dad home-schooled me till I was fifteen, when he died. He said I was way ahead of kids my age back in the States. I'd like to go to school, there's so much to learn."

"You could go with me in New Mexico."

"I'd like that, if I go."

Wow. She's tough. I can't get her to say she'll go. I don't know what I'll do if she won't. In the jungle, she learned how to move without being seen or heard, how to pass through a forest without leaving a sign and how to find food to survive. She probably did most of that on her own, after her dad and mom died.

Hey, I'll be seeing my mom and dad in a couple days.

"We need some food," Jake said. "Any ideas?"

"I think there's an animal trail down to the river part way through the mangroves. Let's work our way through and wait for a tapir to come for a drink. A small one would be just right."

They doused the fire and grabbed their weapons. They picked their way around the enormous root systems where they found a narrow track that ended between two of the largest mangroves. Chanti selected a hidden spot to hole up. They squatted on their heels. An hour later, muffled hoof beats alerted them to the approach of a tapir, or, perhaps a boar. Chanti had a clear view of the trail. When a medium sized tapir materialized, she drew her arrow back and let it fly in one smooth movement. She did not appear to aim. The shaft flew to its mark in a blur. A heart shot. The tapir dropped to its far side, dead before it hit the ground.

Jake gutted the animal and slung it over his shoulder. They retraced their steps to the new camp, built another fire and roasted a big slab of meat. After eating, they hung the remainder in a tree.

"Jake, did you hear that?"

"Sounded like a human scream."

The tormented cry again rang through the trees. Jake couldn't pinpoint where it came from.

Once more the wild, wailing cry echoed through the trees.

Snatching up their weapons, they set off toward the scream. Chanti led the way. She swung her machete as little as possible and glided through the rain forest without sound. Jake followed. He now stalked through the underbrush as silently as Chanti.

"It sounds like a girl's voice. She's calling out in Maya, 'Someone. Help me.'"

They edged closer. Jake caught the scent of sweat.

A crackling of brush.

The slap of a hand on flesh.

An anguished cry.

They crept through the underbrush. Pausing in the middle of a dense thicket, Jake spotted movement ahead.

"There," Jake pointed through a cluster of trees. A terrified young Indian girl struggled against two men. Rage flooded through Jake at the sight of the men abusing the girl. "Let's move in closer."

The two of them wormed their way backward from the thicket until it was safe to stand.

Jake crept from tree to tree. Chanti stepped up to his side, her expression grim, white knuckles gripping her bow and arrow. Together they narrowed the distance without sound. Chanti stopped and raised her hand.

Smoke filled Jake's nostrils. He followed Chanti's gaze. Three other men sat around a fire maybe fifty feet away.

Now what? 5 to 2 isn't good odds.

Chanti changed direction to avoid the camp and arrive at the spot where the two men had the girl trapped. Being outnumbered, extreme care was necessary. Silence would be their ally. No reason to alert the threesome at the fireside.

Thirty feet from the struggle, they dropped to their knees. They crept another fifteen feet closer, avoiding tangled roots and vines. Watching the struggling, terrified girl, Jake wanted to forget his caution.

Those scum. I can't let this happen. Jake's teeth ground together as he glanced over at Chanti. *She feels the same way.*

A sharp thorn jabbed his side. He jumped, thinking it was a knife, but realized in time what it was.

From where they crouched, the girl and her attackers appeared in plain view. Jake clasped his machete in his trembling right hand.

The two men before them were mestizos, a cross between Spanish and Indian, or pure Indians, but not the short-statured Maya. The taller of the two, with a jutting jaw and great gaps in his yellow-brown teeth, squeezed the girl's throat in his hand. Long greasy black hair hung down around his unshaven, scarred face.

He had forced her onto her back while the other man pinned her shoulders to the ground. Shorter, the other man looked much the same, wearing Mexican campesino clothes of baggy pants, cotton shirt and sandals. Both were filthy.

The girl looked a lot like the Lacandons Jake had recently spent time with when visiting Chanti's grandmother. Her sweet face twisted in terror. Jake's temples pounded and his hands shook. Chanti's face was flushed.

The only clothing the girl still wore was a wraparound red skirt now hiked up around her waist. She had full breasts that, as yet, were unaffected by gravity. She was probably thirteen or fourteen years old. The tall man's trousers were lying around his ankles as he knelt in front of her.

As he released her throat to drop his shorts, her shoulder-length black hair flipped as she flung her head from side to side. She let out a shrill, agonized scream. He slapped her hard across her face, rocking her head to the side, and forced her legs apart.

Jake tensed, coiled, ready to spring, so furious, he could hardly contain himself.

A third man approached, cracking loose branches under his feet, and stopped to watch. Big, he leaned against a tree. More formidable than the rapist, he held a long knife low in his hand. His teeth gleamed in a direct ray of sunlight as he leaned against a tree. A line was forming.

We can't wait much longer.

Jake paused, jaw rigid. Sweat poured off him. There were still two more men by the fire.

27

Jake remembered what Uncle Al, a Marine, had once told him. "If several men attack at the same time, you have to move like lightning, hit fast and keep moving."

He glanced at Chanti. She pointed to the man holding the girl's shoulders, then to herself. Jake shook his head and pointed to himself. Pointing to the other, Jake again pointed to himself. Chanti nodded.

She fit an arrow to her bow, nodded toward the third man and held up one finger. He would be the first.

Jake didn't want to use his rifle, because he thought they might get away without alarming the extra men by the fire. But now one of them leaned against a nearby tree.

Next to the fire, shadows moved.

Are they all coming? I'll concentrate on the two with the girl. Chanti can take care of the others.

Her bow drawn, she released the arrow. Jake dashed five steps to the side of the rapist like he was coming out of the starting blocks at the Olympics.

He slammed the butt of his machete's handle into the man's head with such fury, the skull caved in. The opposite side of his head bulged out as he flopped to the ground.

Jake spun toward the other man and leaped over the girl as the man yanked his hands back, reaching for a belted knife.

The girl rolled to her knees and jumped to her feet.

Jake rammed into the man, head butting him in his nose, flattening it. His machete swung up and down, handle smacking into the rapist's forehead. So charged up from anger and adrenaline, he again punched a hole in an enemy's head.

He flipped his machete to his left hand and drew his pistol. Crouching, he wheeled to face the third man.

The man was down on his back, an arrow jutting from his eye.

A fourth clutched the feathered shaft protruding from his chest as he dropped his rifle and pitched backwards.

The fifth man aimed his rifle at Chanti. Jake yelled, "Hey!" and fired.

The shell punched into the man's right arm, shattering it. The weapon clattered onto the rocks.

"Thanks, Jake."

Chanti spoke Maya in a calm voice to the sobbing girl, hiding behind a tree. The young Lacandon replied in a shaky voice. She stepped out from the tree, trembling. Chanti's calm was contagious. She walked to the girl, still talking. She gently hugged her and held her that way as the tears streamed down the girl's cheeks.

The wounded man screamed in pain. Adrenalin still pumping, Jake ripped the attacker's shirt off, tore it up and used it as a tourniquet to staunch the flow of blood, holding his breath as long as possible from the man's overpowering stench. Using a stout piece of wood for a lever, he thrust it through the double knot. Showing the man how to twist the tourniquet tighter, he tied the loose ends around it in another square knot to keep it from loosening. He fashioned a sling from the rest of it.

"They killed her husband. They'd only been married a couple weeks. These men're part of a larger group capturing animals to sell illegally," Chanti said. The girls continued talking.

Jake strode to the fire and smothered it with dirt. He looked through a poacher's backpack and found a relatively clean shirt. Walking back to the girls, he held it out to them. Chanti took the shirt and helped the girl get into it. Jake stripped off the smaller man's sandals for her. Better than nothing. He rolled the man over and bound his hands and feet with the rope belt he wore. He still lived.

"Thanks, Jake."

"Ask her how near the other hunters are."

Chanti and the girl spoke again.

"She says they went on to Chanal, which is where we're headed. She lives in a tiny village of three families a short distance up river. We'll take her there. Okay?"

"Of course. Does she want anything these men had, weapons, clothes, food?"

After a brief discussion, Chanti said, "Maybe a good rifle and ammunition, a knife or two."

Jake gathered the best weapons and used the pack he'd found to carry all but two rifles. He shouldered them separately. While he gathered weapons, Chanti went through the trouser pockets of each man and collected all their pesos. She added them to the girl's new pack. Chanti touched the girl's arm and motioned toward the river. They retraced their steps and found their camp. Now that the action was over, Jake felt wobbly and heavy hearted as he trekked back.

"Her name's Lupita," Chanti said. "She says we're both very brave and she thanks you. We'll always have a friend here."

"I'm sorry we couldn't stop them sooner."

Chanti nodded and said, "Let's build a fire and feed Lupita so she can catch her breath before we move on."

"I'll get the meat down."

Chanti built another small fire and they roasted more of the tapir. Lupita had not eaten for a day. She and Chanti chattered away in Maya.

Jake sat on a log, head bent. He had finished eating. He stared at nothing.

"Jake. Are you all right?"

Chanti squatted in front of him, looking up into his eyes. Jake blinked, then sucked in a huge breath and let it out. He shook his head. She put her hands on his knees. His face relaxed and his eyes softened.

"I'm just feeling down, having to take more lives. I was furious when I attacked. It made me physically stronger than normal and I hit those men too hard. What's wrong with people like that? They might even have daughters her age. How can they do that? I know they were bad men, but I don't feel any better now. I just feel drained. It's hard sometimes to know what's right and wrong."

"I forget that you're not as used to the jungle's ways as I am. You've adapted so quickly. But we had no choice. Look at what a nice young woman we saved. Can that be wrong? Besides, your heart's in the right place. Look what you did for the wounded man."

"You're right. Okay, I'm through pouting."

Darkness descended over the campsite. Jake gave his hammock to Lupita and lay down in the dugout. Uncomfortable was putting it mildly. He dozed off enough to get some rest. The night creatures kept him awake as much as the hard boat. He had lots of time to think about the "law of the jungle." Concentrating on the good aspects, like Lupita instead of the rapists, he created a warm feeling that spread throughout his entire body.

At daybreak, all three rose. Jake cooked the rest of the meat while Chanti and Lupita scouted for fruit. They brought mangos and shate, a soft red, very sweet fruit. Enough remained of the meat and fruit for another meal later.

"Lupita's feeling better. She's over her shock and knows she did everything possible. She can hold her head up," Chanti said.

As they doused the fire and struck camp, Chanti said, "Lupita said the hunters captured a large black jaguar. What if it's Ba lam? I need to know. If it is, I have to free him."

"If they're going to Chanal, we'll find them there. Let's get started."

"I'll explain to Lupita why we're in a hurry." She and Lupita spoke rapidly in Maya. "She understands. She thinks the poachers'll be there today or tomorrow and will probably stay a few days. They have other animals to sell, but can't take them into San Cristobal."

With the boat loaded and Lupita and her gear resting in the middle, they launched onto what should be the last leg of Jake's long journey from the kidnapping attempt.

What else can happen? I'm glad we ran into Lupita, not just to help her, but if that's Ba lam, we can't let anything happen to him.

Jake's face grew flushed and he clenched his teeth. He checked each weapon.

"Hey, Jake. Let's paddle."

As they settled into their rhythm, Lupita reached up and picked two dangling fruits from an overhanging branch. The river here was narrow and it was difficult to stay out from under the many branches.

"That's zapote mamey," Chanti said. "Very good."

Within an hour, Lupita blurted several rapid-fire sentences to Chanti. As they rounded a curve, she half stood and pointed. The dugout rocked, but Jake and Chanti balanced it. Set back in the trees stood a few typical Lacandon thatched roof huts. Half a dozen Indians milled about and walked down to the water's edge to watch them.

"Lupita says the woman in the yellow dress is her mother. She doesn't see her father."

Lupita called out to her mom. Jake guided the canoe into a tiny dock jutting out from the shore with two dugouts tied to it. Their boat coasted to the dock's end and Chanti secured it to an empty post with the bowline.

Their passenger leaped to the dock and dashed to her mom. Tears ran down both faces as they embraced. Two of the men helped Chanti from the dugout and Jake handed up Lupita's pack and the two rifles. The men stroked the rifles with their hands as they examined them. Jake stepped up onto the dock and waited.

Lupita led her mom by the hand to meet them. The mother threw her arms around Chanti and chattered in Maya. Chanti responded and pointed to Jake. The mother hugged Jake, too, still talking. She smelled like cocoa. Lupita followed, hugging Chanti and Jake.

"I've told them that we have to get to Chanal. You ready?"

"Sure. I really hope it's not Ba lam."

They waved and boarded the dugout once more. Untying the bowline, Chanti shoved the boat into the river. Both waved a last time as they settled into their routine. When Jake looked back before they rounded a curve in the river, Lupita still waved from the dock.

Another person I'll never see again. I guess I should just be happy I had the opportunity to help her. I'll never take my easy life for granted again.

An hour later a high waterfall blocked their passage. Unloading their gear and weapons, they fought their way through the jungle to a point above the falls. Returning, they shouldered the dugout and staggered up the hill. After reaching the top, they took a break to refuel, wolfing down the remaining food.

Once back in the water, they continued their trip upriver, Chanti pointed out a small town set up on a hill.

"I think it's name is El Niz," she said. "Another mile or two and we'll leave the river. Notice how much cooler it is here in the mountains. Tonight it'll be cold."

Approaching an ancient wooden dock, Chanti pointed and Jake cut the canoe in. They disembarked and unloaded. Dragging the boat up into the brush, they turned it upside down and camouflaged it.

"We'll make good time to Chanal. You can see the cleared path. Ready?" Chanti said.

"Let's go."

"Chanal's small, but has resisted the government's efforts to subdue the Zapatistas. They're even unfriendly to the Catholic Bishop. We're about thirty miles from San Cristobal, so if you need to get to your mom right away, you can probably hitch a ride or take a bus. If the hunters have Ba lam, I'll take care of it. Don't worry."

"If they're like everybody else we've run into, you'll need help. I won't leave you."

With their packs on and weapons in hand, they jogged the two miles to the town. Nearing the outskirts, they came to a dirt road that led into Chanal. Following it at a rapid pace, they rounded a bend.

And stopped dead.

In a field off to the right sat an encampment of numerous flatbed trucks containing cages filled with animals, birds and reptiles.

A large, black cat paced two steps to one end of its cage, did an about face and repeated the motion.

Over and over.

Never still.

28

The idea of Ba lam caged depressed Jake. There was something sad about so graceful and powerful a wild animal being caged. Especially Ba lam.

Chanti's jaw clenched. Blood rushed to her head. Her hand showed white knuckles wrapped around her machete.

"That's not right, caging all these wild animals," she said. "It looks like Ba lam, but I have to get closer to be sure."

Jake scanned the field. At least five workers tramped the grounds feeding the animals and cleaning up. All wore pistols strapped to their belts. Several rifles lay within easy reach, leaning against the trucks or trees on the edge of the clearing. The workers looked much like the hunters who tried to rape Lupita.

"Let's go back to the tree line and circle around this field to come in from the other side," Jake said.

He gave her a tug and led the way. She was tense, her down-turned mouth frozen stiff. On the far side, they stopped closer to the caged feline.

"Ba lam," Chanti whispered.

He wheeled in the pen's tiny space and faced Chanti. A low rumble burst from his throat. His tongue lolled from the side of his mouth. Ba lam's rounded ears perked up and faced Chanti.

"It's him. I'm positive. Let's get him out of there."

"Wait. There're too many guns around. Ba lam might get hit, or us. We need a plan."

"You're right. Let's watch a while. How many do you see?"

"Five. But there could easily be more. I'll stay here. You speak the language. Why don't you take a walk nearby and ask the locals some questions about these people?"

"Good idea. Back soon."

Chanti faded into the forest and Jake took a closer look at the trucks and cages. Besides Ba lam, two snarling pumas peered through their barred cages from the same flatbed. Another truck contained the pens for two crocodiles and a pair of boas. Behind that truck, cages holding toucans and scarlet macaws rested on another. A fourth carried spider and the dark howler monkeys.

Jake kept his eyes on the men working. Another joined the original five. Four of them were probably truck drivers. As yet, the boss had not shown up.

An hour later, Chanti slipped in beside him holding a paper sack and a three-foot bolt cutter.

"Find out anything?"

"There're six workers and the boss, who went into San Cristobal this morning in a pickup. He frightens a lot of people. Mean. And big. He's been here before and has a bad reputation with the locals."

"I counted six, too. Probably after dark we'll be able to sneak in and free Ba lam. Look at him. Ever since he heard your voice, he's been lying there watching."

"Thanks for staying. I know you want to see your parents."

"No problem. I'd hate myself if something happened to Ba lam or you and I might have helped prevent it."

"I had some pesos so I bought some tamales and bottled water," Chanti said. "Talking to a local about setting Ba lam free got me the loan of this bolt cutter. No one likes these people."

They split the tamales and each gulped down a bottle of water.

"We have a couple hours till dark. You take a nap now and I'll take one after," she said.

Jake used his pack as a pillow and fell asleep. It seemed he had just taken a few z's when Chanti shook him by the shoulder.

"My turn. You were right about the cold. It's freezing compared to the lowlands."

Jake watched until dark and woke her.

"The boss hasn't shown up. Four of the men left to go to town. This is probably a good time to do it. I think we should let all the animals go free. You agree?"

"Yeah. We'd better leave our packs and weapons in case we have to run. Silence and speed. If we do have to run, whether it's before we set him free or after, head back here. If Ba lam's free, we can vanish into the jungle. In any case, we can arm ourselves."

Jake removed his knife and sheath from his belt, lifted his trouser leg and slipped it onto his inside lower right leg. He used a piece of rope to tie it below his knee and smoothed the cloth down over it. Chanti smiled.

"The two poachers who're left have a fire going by the truck cab where the crocs and snakes are. It's not far from Ba lam, but it's not right next to him, either," Jake said. "Those cages all have locks on them. The bolt cutter'll make it easier."

Jake slipped away toward Ba lam. Chanti glided up and whispered Ba lam's name.

In the darkness, a faint gleam, a refection from the nearby fire, came from his eyes. When they got close, the big cat crouched watching them.

Chanti vaulted onto the back of the flatbed and reached through the cage's bars to rub his massive head. A deep cough rasped from him. One of the pumas growled, banging his head on his cage's bars.

Leaping up alongside Chanti, Jake clutched the bolt cutters.

A glaring light blinded them.

A voice said, "Buenas noches, señor, señorita,"

Chanti and Jake spun in their squatting position to face the new threat. Ba lam snarled. Both dropped to the ground and stood four feet from the three men.

Two pointed rifles at them and the third a pistol. The closer rifleman had a barrel-shaped body with short arms and legs. He had slanted eyes, a wide blunt nose and big lips. The second rifleman held the blinding torch and it was difficult to see what he looked like, except he was short like the other.

The speaker, pistol pointed at Jake and Chanti, stood in the middle. Taller than Jake, a big belly hung over his belt. His short-sleeved shirt showed thick, muscular arms. Relatively clean compared to the other two, his black hair and mustache were neatly trimmed.

"You look like an American," he said to Jake. "Do you speak English?"

"Right."

"What are you doing with my cats?"

"This black jaguar is mine," Chanti said. "I've come to release him."

"Have you, now. I don't think so. We went to a lot of trouble to catch these animals. They're worth too much money."

Chanti had an edge to her voice, warning Jake something was going to happen. She stepped up closer to the big man.

"You're two or three times as big as me, but I'm still standing up to you. Either I'm crazy or I'm really dangerous. Maybe both. Do you want to find out?"

The two short men stepped up on either side of Jake and grabbed his upper arms. Both had powerful grips and he would have a hard time breaking free from their vice-like holds.

Smiling pleasantly, the big man sauntered toward Chanti. She stayed still, impassive. He couldn't read her. She was ice, betraying no emotion.

Gun at his side, completely confident, the man stepped up face to face with her.

He grabbed her arm with his free hand, spinning her around away from him and yanked her right arm behind her. She offered no resistance and he smiled.

Reaching around her, he grabbed her breast.

Chanti exploded.

She lifted her foot, knee into her chest, bellowed and stomped down hard on his instep using her heel.

It broke something in the bridge of his foot. Ba lam snarled and crashed against the bars.

The poacher cried out in pain and released her.

She turned into the thief and brought her elbow up against the bridge of his nose. Crack! The cartilage broke. Blood gushed from his nostrils as though from a spigot.

His legs buckled. His gun dropped.

He tried to back away from her, but his foot gave out. When he put his weight on it, he stumbled, needing to plant his other foot to save him from falling.

Crazy with pain, he gritted his teeth and made an effort to lunge toward her, determined to make her pay.

"You bitch. I'll kill you slowly when I'm done with you."

He was mistaken if he thought he could frighten her.

Enraged, Chanti ran straight into him, head butting him in his forehead, and with a sudden adrenaline burst, grabbed his shirtfront with both hands, screamed and smashed her forehead into his broken nose, crushing it. Blood splattered over her and covered his face.

He was far more powerful than Chanti and she needed to end it quickly.

Following the head butt, her legs kept pumping, driving her forward. She knocked him backward with all her strength.

His head must have felt like it had burst and he cried out in agony as he toppled to the ground.

His blood-covered face sagged. His eyes widened and his mouth hung open.

For the first time, he realized he was injured and unable to defend himself. Too late.

His head exploded as Chanti drove the toe of her shoe into his temple.

Darkness.

Jake ducked down and drove his arms up as he rose again. The sudden move threw the two astounded men's grips, already loosened, from his arms.

He slashed a backhand at the man on his left, a short hard arc that whipped across his throat. The man's yell ended, instantly. Jake followed it with a hard right to the nose.

The second man grabbed Jake from behind and threw him into the truck's flatbed frame.

Jake's head struck metal and his vision dimmed.

He seemed to be in a long, dark tunnel.

He faced his enemy.

The man charged toward him and Jake pancaked him to his back on the ground.

He slammed his forearm into the man's throat. Gagging, the man fought for breath while Jake raised his pant leg and jerked his knife out.

The first man rose to his feet and raised his rifle that had fallen beside him.

29

No time. The rifle was aimed straight at Jake and his knife had just cleared its leather sheath.

The bolt cutter slashed across the man's hands and rifle, driving it down. A shot fired into the dirt and the rifle clattered to the ground.

The man screamed. Both hands dangled uselessly at the ends of his forearms, like a racehorse that had snapped its leg in half.

Jake gripped the other's throat and held his knife to it. The man stopped struggling. Eyes wide and mouth open, he trembled.

Chanti bashed the broken handed man on the head with the bolt cutter. He pitched to the ground, not even feeling the pain as he fell on his hands.

Breathing hard and hands trembling, she helped Jake bind the conscious man's hands and legs. The other two lay motionless, but still breathing. They bound them, too.

"Lets free all the animals except Ba lam. The San Cristobal airport's on the other side of Chanal, nearer here than San Cristobal. If he's caged, maybe we can fly him to Lacanja, close to home. I know Chan Bor flies up here sometimes from there. How much money do you have?"

"About two thousand pesos, but I can get more if there's an ATM around," Jake said.

"There's probably one at the local bank. If you'll lend me the money, you can go ahead and meet your parents in San Cristobal and I'll come back with the pilot afterwards."

"I think I'd rather go with you," Jake said. *What if she never came back? I'd probably never see her again.* "Maybe we can call my mom from town."

"Good idea. She's probably worried. I'd much rather have you with me. It's kind of scary, since I've never been in a plane."

"Let's let these animals go and head into town," Jake said. He pushed himself onto the flatbed with the bolt cutters and cut the locks on the pumas' two cages. Standing aside, he opened their doors. They fled into the jungle. Jake heaved the two cages to the flatbed's side and dumped them off the truck. He went from truck to truck setting crocodiles, boas, monkeys and birds all free, while Chanti talked to Ba lam.

"Can you drive this truck?" Chanti asked. "I can't drive."

"Sure. I've been driving tractors and trucks on the ranch since I was eleven. We'll take it into town and park it behind a building where it can't be seen. You stay with Ba lam and I'll see about money and a phone call."

Jake jogged back for their packs and weapons, scooped them up and returned. He stuck the packs and his rifle in the truck's cab and handed up Chanti's bow and arrows to her. She had found a two-gallon bucket filled with water for Ba lam. Together, they shoved Ba lam's cage against the cab's back, where it wouldn't be so noticeable. The keys were in the ignition.

He drove to the middle of town, grinding the gears a couple of times, and parked in a narrow street behind the bank. Chanti sat next to Ba lam's cage, stroking him and talking to him. Jake left them in the dark and vanished around the building. Nobody waited at the ATM, so he used his card to extract four thousand pesos, the maximum he could get at one time. He tried again and got an equal amount. He hoped that would be enough. Combined with the two thousand he already had, he now possessed in pesos the equivalent of one thousand dollars.

He found an Internet café still open and had the woman place a call to his mom's hotel in San Cristobal. He got an English speaker who informed him Mr. And Mrs. Brandon weren't in. He left a message that he would probably be there in less than two days.

Following the one sign for San Cristobal, they left Chanal. Ten kilometers down the road, they turned off in the direction of the airport. Jake drove toward a lighted office where he saw a small plane parked. He braked and pulled up in front. As he climbed from the cab, Chanti dropped beside him. He tried the door and it opened. Not too late.

A hanging shaded light bulb over a desk provided the only light. Papers, books and magazines littered every surface including the floor. Behind the desk sat a man with a black patch covering his right eye. He smiled as Chanti stepped up to the desk. Unshaven, he looked piratical but rumpled. A New York Yankees' baseball cap sat at an angle on his long curly hair. His age could have been anywhere from 50 to 70.

Chanti asked, "Do you speak English?"

"Of course." He stood up, almost as tall as Jake, slim and a busted-up face. "I lived in California for a while and spent some time flying for the US forces in Vietnam. What can I do for you?"

"We have a caged jaguar we want to return to Lacanja country. Can you take us?"

"Maybe tomorrow I can. What would you be doing with a jaguar? That's illegal. I could lose my license."

"We'll trade you the truck for the flight and a ride to San Cristobal when we get back," Jake said.

"The truck and five thousand pesos for the risk I'm taking."

"Three thousand."

"Four and it's a deal."

"Okay. Can we leave in the morning?"

"Sure. Let's see the cage's size."

They walked out to the truck. He pushed himself stiffly up onto the flatbed and looked closely at the cage. Ba lam snarled and swiped at the bars. The man jumped back.

"He's a big one. I think we can get this in my Cessna. I'll pull out the back seats. One of you will have to sit on the deck. I'll take out the seats tonight and we'll leave at first light. You have the money now?"

Jake counted out four thousand pesos and handed them to the pilot. "My name's Jake and this is Chanti."

"They call me El Tuerto, but my real name's Mario Séneca." The man went to the water dispenser and filled a cup.

Chanti said to Jake, "El Tuerto means one-eyed."

"Aww. You speak Spanish. You from Mexico?" said El Tuerto.

"Chiapas. I'm half Lacandon and half American." Chanti brushed hair from her eyes.

"A great mix. Want some water?"

They nodded and he poured them two cups.

"You kids want to sleep in the building?" he said, handing them the water.

Chanti angled her head toward Jake. "I'll stay out here with Ba lam. You go inside if you want, Jake."

"I'll sleep out here, too. See you in the morning, El Tuerto." Jake grabbed blankets El Tuerto handed him.

"Okay. I'll be working on the plane for a while. Don't let me bother you."

El Tuerto turned and vanished into the office. Jake and Chanti pulled their packs and weapons from the cab and boosted themselves onto the flatbed. They made a nest next to Ba lam's cage. Chanti spent some time talking to him as he flopped against the bars as close to her as possible. Jake lay at her other side and fell asleep. Noises from the plane didn't keep him awake for a second.

Ba lam growled. Chanti and Jake sat up reaching for their weapons.

Gray light. El Tuerto stood close by.

"Time to start loading," he said. "I've borrowed a forklift from one of the bigger hangers to load the cage. First, I think we should hose it down if your jaguar won't be too insulted."

Chanti said, "Good idea. Use the forklift to haul the cage to the hose and then the plane."

"Have you flown in a small plane before?" El Tuerto said.

"Not even a big one," Chanti said.

Smiling, El Tuerto drove the forklift up to the flatbed's side. With a little maneuvering, he got the fork's blades under the cage and lifted it. Ba lam snarled and crouched. Chanti talked to him as she walked beside the cage. The pilot transported the cage closer to the water spigot at the building's front. Chanti used the hose to clean the cage while Ba lam danced back and forth, constantly growling. She held the hose to his mouth while he drank.

As El Tuerto steered the forklift toward the plane, Chanti and Jake got their first good look at it. The aged looking twin-engine airplane had definitely seen better days. Once white, it boasted chipped faded dark blue and gray accent stripes. More than a few dents showed on the body. The wings were the only things that seemed relatively new. The tires looked bald. It didn't look promising, but their choices were slim.

Jake held the right side door open while El Tuerto took his time and slipped the cage in on his first try. Chanti ran to the far side and entered through that door. When the pilot withdrew the forklift, Chanti and Jake shifted the cage slightly so the doors would close.

As El Tuerto drove the lift back to a nearby hanger, Jake and Chanti had a chance to talk.

"You sit in the front seat," Jake said. "Since this is your first time, you'll be less likely to get airsick there. I'll stay in the back with Ba lam, unless he gets too wild."

"Do you think this thing is safe? It looks pretty beat up," Chanti said.

"Pilot's still alive. We'll soon find out."

Their one-eyed pilot sauntered up.

"The plane is old and looks like junk, but the engine is in superb shape, always in superb shape. Absolutely nothing to worry about," said El Tuerto. "Ready? Who's sitting in front?"

Jake stepped over and opened the door for Chanti. She climbed in stoically.

She must be nervous, but look at her. Doesn't show a thing. It's different when she has to rely on someone else.

Jake and the pilot clambered aboard and the engine kicked in the first try, then hacked and gurgled violently.

El Tuerto glanced right. "Chanti, fasten your seatbelt, please. Jake, help her, won't you."

Jake leaned forward and buckled it into place.

"This is a twin-engine Cessna Beach Baron 58. It normally holds six passengers. I often use it for cargo, so this is nothing new. Any questions before we take off?

Chanti said, "Have you ever crashed?" Her hand came up and swiped back a stray wisp of hair that had escaped from her braid.

El Tuerto chuckled. "Any bush pilot who tells you he hasn't is a liar. I have four children and I've had more plane wrecks than kids. The last one was a close call. Hold on while I take off and then I'll tell you."

Jake gulped. Chanti stared straight ahead, gripping the seat's arms like she was strangling the hunter's boss.

He taxied out to the grass airstrip, revved up the engine several times and sent the small plane streaking down the runway. As the twin-engine Cessna rose from the runway, El Tuerto banked the plane to the left.

His door flew open.

Jake clutched the cage with a death grip. Chanti gripped her seat's arms with white knuckles.

"I guess I'll have to get that fixed one of these days," El Tuerto said, as he leaned far out, reaching with his left hand, trying to steer through the upward arc of the flight with his right.

He grabbed the door and slammed it shut as the plane veered downward toward the trees below.

"Whoops!" El Tuerto pulled back on the yoke and leveled the aircraft before taking it skyward again. The Cessna gurgled and for a breathtaking second, a funeral home-like silence engulfed them before El Tuerto yanked it back to sputtering life.

This was Chanti's first time in a plane. She was getting an education. It wasn't helping Jake's nerves much, either.

"To continue my story, I was coming back from a delivery like this. I felt like my chest had exploded. I tried to scream, but no sound came out. I blacked out and my plane was going down. I regained consciousness long enough to pull the plane up and make a bumpy landing on a river, hitting the water flat to slow down and bouncing onto the stony shoreline stopping a half foot from a tree trunk. Luckily, some Indians saw it and took me to a doctor. I had a heart attack, but I'm fine now." He chuckled again and broke into a hearty laugh.

We must be as crazy as he looks. I doubt we'll ever get there alive.

Aloud, Jake said, "Maybe you don't belong in the sky if you keep falling out of it."

Chanti frowned, alarmed, and reached back to touch Jake's hand. Their eyes locked.

Land vanished as the Cessna skimmed up over a jagged ridge top. Jake's stomach dropped. In the dizzying plummet that followed, Chanti let out a yell.

30

A smile formed on the one-eyed pilot's unshaven face. The agile Cessna swooped down the mountainside and leveled off.

"Sorry. I couldn't resist that."

"I'd appreciate it if you didn't kill my jaguar before we get there," Chanti gasped, still hanging on to the seat.

"If you do that again, I'm gonna open the cage," Jake said.

Ba lam lay on his stomach, front paws hooked around two bars in the cage. He snarled and gnashed his teeth over and over.

El Tuerto threw his head back and laughed. "Okay. Okay. I'll behave."

Mountains jutted up everywhere looking like an ocean of green waves. Small rivers flowed through the valleys. Tiny village clearings lay scattered throughout the forest. An occasional column of smoke drifted up from a cooking fire and disappeared. Chanti's eyes widened and her mouth hung open as she watched the panorama laid out below.

"It sure looks different from up here. I don't recognize anything," Chanti said.

A little stream of smoke flowed out behind the right engine's cowling, which was patched with silver and blue aluminum squares.

"What's with the smoke?" Jake asked.

"Just a little oil seeping through an O-ring. No problem," El Tuerto said.

"Didn't the space shuttle Challenger blow up because of the same problem?" Jake said.

"Hah! So it did," El Tuerto said.

The flight took on another aspect. They started to hit a lot of clouds, which thickened. The wing tips disappeared into the clouds. Jake kept expecting the nose of a large airliner to emerge from the clouds at the moment they crashed into it.

They dropped below the clouds toward a tiny grass airstrip. Jake couldn't believe they were going to land on such a short runway with towering trees at each end. It looked like Ba lam had taken his paw and clawed a short swath through the green.

To land, the Cessna would have to stop within one hundred fifty yards. If not, it would crash into the trees or land in the river. El Tuerto circled the clearing. Laughing, he thrust the yoke forward and the plane, rattling like tin cans, swooped downward.

The air pressure increased in Jake's ears. He swallowed hard.

They cleared the trees with three inches to spare. Maybe four. Jake waited to feel the trees grab the landing gear. Seconds later, El Tuerto pulled back on the yoke and leveled off the plane. As the wheels bounced along the rough grass airstrip, he shouted, "Ahah! Lucky again!"

For a few moments, it didn't look like the Cessna would stop before it plunged over the edge of the river embankment. The aircraft skidded to a standstill ten feet from the brink. Turning the plane, El Tuerto drove off to the side of the runway and stopped.

Chanti and Jake staggered from the plane still dizzy from the fast drop. Sweat oozed from their brows.

The pilot joined them. "Fun, huh?" He laughed. "If you're going to free the big cat, it'll be better to let him go here, away from that building and any people around."

"I'll take Ba lam into the jungle. Jake, will you wait with our ride?" Chanti's voice shook.

I don't think she trusts him to wait for us. And she realizes she may never see Ba lam again.

"Okay. Let's see if we can unload this cage. I'll drag out this end and you two stand on either side of the door and ease it down to the ground," Jake said.

The three of them strained to unload Ba lam's heavy cage. The big cat paced again. Chanti talked to him as she used the bolt cutter she had brought with her and lopped off the padlock. She swung open the door and Ba lam sprinted out, heading for the river. Chanti grabbed her weapons and raced after him.

He paused and looked back at her. She dropped her weapons and leaped on him. They rolled on the ground, wrestling. He gave a throaty warning. Snarling, he allowed her to roll him over on his back. She paused, sitting on his massive chest, and roughed up his head between her hands. Chanti climbed off Ba lam who leaped up beside her. They trotted off together toward the river and vanished over the embankment.

Jake's smile faded. Sadness spread through him. He would probably never see the big cat again.

"I've never seen that before. That young lady's crazier than me," El Tuerto said. "Let's drag this cage over to the trees and see if they have anything to eat and drink in the office."

When they entered the building, El Tuerto spoke to the counterman in Spanish. The cadaverous man poured two cups of coffee and reached under the counter. He brought up two burritos.

"Jake, do you have 100 pesos for the man?"

"We need a burrito for Chanti, too. And coffee when she gets back." Jake handed the man behind the counter a two hundred peso note. The timeworn man forgot to make change and poured whiskey into El Tuerto's cup.

Burrito and coffee in hand, Jake strolled outside to recover from the hair-raising flight. He sat on a rough wooden bench, leaned back against the building's wall and nibbled at his burrito. Finished with the food and coffee, he dozed off.

Chanti shook him awake. He judged by the sun's position he had been asleep for a couple hours.

"Ba lam's okay. He was his old self when I left him. I think he's pretty hungry. He's probably hunting right now. If he doesn't find something, he will tonight. That's his favorite time to hunt, anyway. He drank gallons from the river."

"Hope he'll be okay. I didn't even get a chance to say good-bye, he took off so fast. Maybe he'll find a mate. Let's see if our pilot's ready to go. I want to see my mom, now that everything's taken care of. Dad, too. I just added up how many days I've been gone since they tried to kidnap me. This is the tenth day."

They entered the building and Jake gave Chanti her burrito while the counter man poured her coffee and topped off Jake's cup.

"You ready?" Jake asked El Tuerto.

"Soon as she finishes."

After a quick bathroom stop, the trio walked back to the plane. The pilot eased the Cessna up to a pump and filled the tank, then steered them back to the runway's end.

Hope he didn't drink too much. He's skillful, but I don't see how he can get us into the air over those trees. They're too close.

"Here we go," El Tuerto yelled as the Cessna streaked down the runway.

We're going to run straight into those trees. There's no possible way to miss them.

But they cleared the skyscraping treetops by inches. And away they soared.

This time, Jake sat in the co-pilot's seat with Chanti sitting on a pack in the rear. She leaned as close to a window as she could get. She and Jake watched the scenery drift by. Lush, green jungle everywhere. A mist covered waterfall, a green lagoon, big rivers and smaller ones, an Indian village.

The plane's nose dipped, at first slightly and then sharply.

Jake jerked his head toward El Tuerto. The pilot's head was nodding and his chin sank to his chest. Sound asleep or a heart attack?

He slumped into the yoke, jammed it forward and and the Cessna dove straight down.

The ground rushed toward them.

Jake grabbed the back of "One-eyed's" shirt and jerked him into an upright position.

"Help me," he said to Chanti. "Hold him there."

He seized the controls.

What next? He better be just asleep and not dead.

After Jake yanked back on the yoke, he wrenched with all his strength to bring the instrument's horizon level. They had dived into a valley or he would never have pulled the nose up in time.

I've just exhausted my total knowledge of flying. Uh, oh. Mountainside coming up.

Jake dragged back hard on the yoke, sending the plane toward the jagged pinnacle. His heart pounded and his hands were slippery with sweat.

Even without El Tuerto, it missed the ridgetop. Inches to spare.

He reached over and shook El Tuerto, who responded groggily. Jake slapped him across the back of his head to bring him to full alertness.

Guessing what must have happened, El Tuerto said, "Hey. I feel better after my nap. I have the yoke now. You must know how to fly?"

"No. Only from playing video games on Playstation."

"Sorry about that. Shouldn't have had the whiskey."

The rest of the trip slipped by without excitement. Jake and Chanti relaxed after a while. As they approached their destination, the landing strip looked huge compared to the tiny strip in Lacanja. El Tuerto talked to someone on the radio as he circled the field, swooped in on one of several landing strips and eased the tires onto the runway without a jolt.

He taxied to his pint-sized building and parked the Cessna.

"Okay, guys. Let's hit the bathroom and I'll drive you into San Cristobal in my new truck." He trotted through the door and straight to the men's room.

"That man's crazy," Chanti said. "How is he still alive?"

"He said you were crazier than him when he saw you wrestling Ba lam."

"Oh, thanks." Chanti punched Jake's shoulder. "You'll be seeing your folks in a couple hours. I don't see how anything else can slow us down."

"I feel guilty, now. It didn't bother me much before, but Mom's probably been plenty worried," Jake said. "I hope you two like each other."

El Tuerto strode out the door. "Next."

Jake motioned for Chanti to go. When she returned, he took his turn. They loaded the truck's cab and jumped in, Chanti in the middle and El Tuerto behind the wheel. He drove the truck out onto the frontage road and in a couple minutes they were out of the airport onto the main road to San Cristobal.

"This thing runs okay," El Tuerto said. "Good deal. Let's see if it can keep up with that train."

Chanti and Jake had not noticed the train off to the left. El Tuerto's handling of the truck interested them more. He floored the accelerator. Nothing happened. Then, bit-by-bit, it picked up speed.

"There're some nasty looking guys behind us. Friends of yours?" El Tuerto said.

Chanti said, "Don't look now, but they're our friends, the poachers."

Jake craned his neck to look back. Another flatbed cruised along behind, gaining on them. The cab held three men. The big one on the passenger side wore bandages on his face. Four more men stood leaning against the back of the cab, rifles in hand.

"Keep this thing floored," Jake shouted. "I can't believe this. I thought we were home free."

"We'll make it. Don't worry," Chanti said, putting her arm around his shoulders. "Better get our weapons ready, though."

The truck bounced over pothole after pothole. Jake's head hit the ceiling.

"You could try to miss one of those," he said.

Their truck held its own against their pursuers. El Tuerto kept glancing to his left at the train.

Three shots cracked behind them. Jake ducked. They missed.

What's that crazy one-eyed man thinking of now?

In the distance, the railroad tracks crossed the main road.

He can't be racing the train to the crossing. We'll never make it. This truck won't go that fast.

El Tuerto hunched over the steering wheel like a jockey whipping his mount down the stretch.

"Hawww! Vámonos, Baby," he screamed.

31

Jake caught his breath.

Chanti's arm tightened around him. Her iron grip threatened to crush his shoulder. Jake hunched forward like El Tuerto. "Come on, Baby," he screamed.

Their truck gained enough ground so it raced nose to nose with the long freight train's two back-to-back engines.

The crossing flew toward them. The red signal lights blinked.

The train's whistle blared.

Jake glanced back. The poacher's truck no longer gained on them, but two of the men aimed their rifles again.

This time, when the shots sounded, Jake didn't duck. The trucks bounced too much for accurate shooting.

The whistle blasted again. Grinning, El Tuerto never hesitated. He kept the gas pedal floored.

They raced toward the intersection one hundred yards ahead. Their truck had gained a little more on the train.

If we only had a longer stretch, we might make it. It'll be close.

Jake and Chanti held hands. He leaned toward her and kissed her cheek. His stomach churned. She nuzzled his face and smiled.

I'm with two insane people. Look at them smiling.

As they drew within twenty yards, the railroad track's curve into the roadway provided the buffer they needed. The engines needed seconds longer to reach the crossing because of it.

The truck bounced over the track with as much to spare as El Tuerto's clearance of the trees in his plane. Three inches. Maybe four.

"Yeah! Lucky again," El Tuerto screamed. He sat back and laughed, tears flowing down his cheeks.

Jake and Chanti joined him. They hugged each other.

El Tuerto pushed the truck at top speed to put as much distance between them and the hunters as possible. The long freight train still crossed the road as they swept over a hill and down to a valley.

"I'm glad you guys found me," said the one-eyed driver. "I haven't had so much fun in years." He chuckled, wiping his cheeks with the back of his hand.

"We've grown to appreciate you even if you are crazy," Jake said. "I'm headed to see my parents and we might not have made it if you weren't driving. Now, it looks like we will."

"We want to go to the Rincón del Arco Hotel a few blocks from the zócalo. Know it?" Chanti said.

"Yep. On Ejército Nacional. Nice old hotel. Won't be long, now. You can see the outskirts of San Cristobal ahead."

"You'll like my mom, Chanti. Dad, too."

"Your mom sounded nice on the phone. Too bad you couldn't talk to them from Chanal."

"Soon, now. Nothing can stop us this time."

El Tuerto said, "Here's a great view of San Cristobal. I love to fly over this city. It's one of

Chiapas's most beautiful. See how it sits in this highland valley surrounded by forests. It's almost 7,500 feet above sea level."

The mountain highway wasn't for timid drivers, full of switchbacks and steep drop-offs. El Tuerto drove like he flew. He careened around sharp curves with 2,000 foot drop-offs and no guard rail. Chanti's grin joined his.

"This is as good as running the rapids," she said. "Wow. Look at that. Straight down."

"Maybe I spoke too soon," Jake said. "Maybe I'll never see my mom and dad again."

"You can see the tall steeple in the middle of town. It's the Temple of Santo Domingo and sits right on the edge of the zócalo or Plaza Cívica," El Tuerto said.

Minutes later, the truck coasted to a slower speed as they entered traffic.

Locals and tourists crowded the streets. Shops, restaurants and color surrounded the central zócalo, packed with trees and flowering red, lavender and white bougainvilleas. Old Maya men and women, as well as young blond tourists, filled the plaza's benches. Street performers, balloon venders, couples and kids strolled the sidewalks. Live music blared. San Cristobal blended Spanish Colonial influences, the ancient Maya and modern tourism.

For once, El Tuerto drove sanely. The truck braked to a stop in front of a colonial hotel in one of the oldest neighborhoods in San Cristobal de las Casas. Lush gardens filled with flowering plants, cactus and trees grew throughout the grounds.

Jake grasped Chanti's hand. She smiled and looked into his eyes. A red flush spread up through his neck and face. She squeezed his hand.

They climbed from the cab, lugging their belongings with them. El Tuerto stood next to them, admiring the hotel.

"Nice, huh," he said.

"Thanks for everything, El Tuerto," Jake said. "Hope you don't run into those guys on your way back."

"No problem. They'll never know what hit them."

"I love your driving and you're not a bad pilot, either, although I hope you quit falling from the sky," Chanti said. She reached up and hugged him.

"Adiós, my friends," El Tuerto said as he clambered behind the steering wheel.

Jake shook his head, smiling. "It'll probably be a long time before we meet anyone like him again, if ever."

He and Chanti strolled up the flag stoned walkway and entered the lobby. Wooden and leather furniture and colorful serapes with deep reds and browns appointed a warm reception area. They passed a cozy restaurant and bar as they strode up to the desk.

Jake smiled ear to ear at the pretty receptionist.

"My name's Jake Brandon. Could you call my mom, Sharon Brandon, to tell her I'm here?"

"One moment, please. The manager would like to speak to you."

A chill dampened Jake's warm spirits.

She walked back to a closed door, knocked and stepped inside. A thin, neatly groomed man in his thirties stepped out two minutes later.

"Please come in, Sr. Brandon," he motioned for them to come to his office.

As Jake and Chanti sat in the two visitor's chairs, the manager sat across his desk from them.

"This is Chanti Alexander," Jake said.

"Are you related to Martin Alexander?"

"His daughter. I stayed here with him three years ago."

"A fine man. My name is Francisco de Alba. To get right to the point, I'm afraid I have bad news."

Jake's blood ran cold. He had a knot in his stomach. Chanti gripped his arm.

"Both your parents have been kidnapped by the Zapatistas. Apparently, your father's magazine printed an article that offended them. They are asking the magazine for a ransom. I have called the police chief to let him know you are here and he should arrive any minute. He will be able to explain everything to you. For now, your parents are unharmed to our knowledge."

"Where were they kidnapped from?" Jake asked.

"Here. In this hotel. I was off duty at the time, so I don't know the details."

A knock at the door and it opened to let in a uniformed overweight man. His mustache and belly hanging over his belt reminded Jake of another man he had met in the jungle.

"Buenas tardes, señor Brandon. My name is Jaime Diaz. I'm the Chief of Police."

"And this is my friend, Chanti Alexander," Jake said.

The manager pulled up another chair for the chief.

"Please tell me what happened and what we can do," Jake said, his voice trembling.

"The kidnapping happened yesterday evening. Six men, wearing black balaclavas, rough blankets and open sandals of guerilla fighters, left with your parents under guard. They were all armed. The ransom notice received at your father's magazine office claimed they were Zapatistas. They must have entered the hotel without masks and weapons showing, dressed like civilians. They probably donned their masks once they reached Mr. and Mrs. Brandon's room."

"Were my parents uninjured when they left?" Jake said.

"Yes. The entire police force is on a state of alert. The soldiers stationed nearby are scouring the surrounding countryside. It's a tough job because much of the rough terrain is covered with impenetrable vegetation. So far, no sign of them."

Jake didn't know where to look for his parents, but he was prepared to search the jungle from end to end to find them. He had no doubts about their danger after the brazen kidnapping.

I can't believe after the struggle we had to get here that the Zapatistas kidnapped Mom and Dad. Chanti'll help me get them back.

Now Jake understood what his mom and dad had gone through when he was kidnapped. Shame, because he took so long to contact them, spread through him like hot lava pouring from a volcano. Sweat ran down his brow and his back, soaking his shirt.

The chief continued. "Right now, there's no new information. The soldiers are searching everywhere. Perhaps in the morning. I'll call you then."

"Thank you, Chief," Jake said.

As the chief lumbered out, the manager said, "Your parents arranged rooms for the two of you. Perhaps you would like to clean up?"

"Very much. And we need some new clothes."

"If you will write down what you want and what sizes, I'll send the receptionist and take care of the desk myself. Come. The keys are at the desk."

Jake handed the man 2,000 pesos.

"I have an idea. Let me think about it for a while," Chanti said.

They walked to their side-by-side rooms and indulged themselves in long, hot showers. After they dried, they were surprised to find a stack of clothes and shoes already inside their doors.

Dressed in new jeans, shirt and hiking shoes, Jake knocked on Chanti's connecting door. When he saw her, she took his breath away. Her hair was down and she had a softer look. She didn't look so much like the warrior he knew she was. She also wore new jeans, shirt and running shoes.

"Come in, Jake. Don't worry. We'll find them. I have the beginnings of a plan."

They sat together on a leather sofa. She took his hand in hers.

"When I came here with my dad three years ago, I met a Zapatista. His name's Baltazar Vegas. My dad saved his life when he would have drowned in a river. He said if there's anything he can ever do, he will. I'm going to call him on that promise.

It's too late to do anything tonight, except get in touch with him."

"Do you think he'll be able to do anything? Those are his people."

"I called him just before you came. His name's in the phone book. He's going to meet us in the hotel's restaurant in half an hour. I haven't told him anything except I need a favor. Don't worry. We'll get your parents back safely."

"Thanks, Chanti. I knew I could count on you. I didn't realize what Mom and Dad must have been going through. Stupid me. I was all wrapped up in my own problems and excitement. We'll find a way."

"I'm starved. Let's go down and order some food. When he comes, he can join us."

"Wow, you smell good. I'd forgotten how it feels to be really clean."

"It is nice, isn't it?"

In the restaurant, they ordered seafood, soup and a salad and ice tea. Only one other couple sat on the far side.

A short stocky man entered while they devoured their soup. His farmer's hands, thick forearms and neck, gave him a sturdy look. His short black hair framed strong Maya features. He strode straight to their table. Jake and Chanti stood.

"I'm Chanti Alexander. We met when my father, Martin, was here a few years ago."

"Baltazar Vegas. I remember you well, although you're all grown up now. And beautiful."

"Thank you. This is my friend Jake Brandon."

Baltazar's eyebrows raised in a sign of recognition. "Ah, the Brandons."

"It's because of him that I called you. Please sit down. Will you have something to eat?"

All three sat.

"No, thank you. I will have a coffee, though. Please go on with your meal."

Chanti ordered him a coffee.

"Jake's parent's were kidnapped from here a day ago, apparently by your Zapatistas. We have to get them back. Can you help us?"

"I don't think so. No."

32

"Let me explain," said Baltazar Vegas. "I know of the kidnapping. I'm sorry it was your parents, Jake. The small group that carried out the abduction is a splinter group. They were advised not to proceed, but they did anyway. There are only six of them and I believe I know where they're holding your parents. The best I can do is show you where they probably are. But I can't directly interfere without bringing the wrath of a lot of people down on me."

"Sounds fair," Chanti said. "I don't want to interfere with the EZLN. I think they've done a lot of good. But we still have to get Jake's mom and dad back safely. We'll try to do it without harm to your group."

"Okay, then. I need to find out some more and I'll pick you up in front of the hotel at 10:00AM. Okay?"

"10:00 it is. See you then. And thanks," Jake said. He stood and shook hands.

"Chanti, I do this for you. Your father was a brave man and saved my life. I will still owe you when this is finished. I'm glad to help. Until tomorrow."

He drained his coffee cup, turned and strode from the restaurant. Jake and Chanti finished their meal and strolled back to their rooms.

A half hour later, Jake heard a knock on his door.

"Come on in," Jake said, opening it.

Chanti reclined on the red sofa in front of the TV, Jake joined her.

"What's EZLN?" Jake asked.

"The Zapatista Army of National Liberation. They've been pretty quiet lately. Their armed uprising in '94 got a lot of attention, but the government hasn't changed anything. The villages of the Lacandon forest continue to resist, but they still lack water and electricity. Children still rarely go beyond primary school. The EZLN tries to change that."

"Maybe we can get my mom and dad back without hurting anyone, although it sounds like they're outlaws to their own people. Thanks for helping, Chanti. I'd be lost, not knowing where to turn. Now, if Baltazar points us in the right direction, I know the two of us can get them out."

Jake leaned over and kissed her cheek. She nuzzled his neck and kissed it, sending shivers down his body.

"I'm worn out from the wild rides we had," Chanti said.

She rested against him, head on his shoulder, and he put his arm around her. They leaned back and dozed off.

Jake awoke to light streaming in the window and a stiff arm. The phone was ringing.

Chanti's eyes peered up at him.

Jake spoke briefly to the chief. When he hung up, he said, "No news."

"Don't worry. We'll find them today. I feel better after that rest," Chanti said. "You?"

"Much. Let's have breakfast and come back to get ready. We might as well wear our jungle clothes and take our weapons. I just hope we won't have to use 'em."

They ate juevos rancheros with a spicy salsa and drank horchata, a drink of rice milk mixed with cinnamon, lime juice and sugar.

Chanti put down her fork and looked into Jake's eyes.

"Don't worry. The Zapatistas won't harm them if they don't resist. We'll get them back safe."

"Zapatistas can't be any worse than some of the others we've met in the last eleven days. Should we head back to the room?"

"Sure. We slept in and it'll be 10:00 pretty quick."

With their weapons wrapped in blankets, they waited on the street for Baltazar. He drove to the hotel entrance in a red 4-wheel drive Toyota pickup and they climbed in. After exchanging greetings and driving off, he explained where they were going.

He shifted into fourth and said, "There's a hidden cave in the forest where they probably are. The army would never suspect it's there. I'll drop you off two kilometers away and point out the path leading to their camp. I'll return in two hours, but then, if you're not back, I'll wait until you return with the Brandons. With the army around, I don't want to look suspicious. If you return before, wait for me in hiding. Sound okay with you?"

"Perfect. You're very kind," Chanti said.

"You're both very young. What makes you think you can take on these men?"

Jake said, "We have to. No other choice."

He nodded and smiled for the first time.

They rode in silence deep into the forest. Baltazar pulled over at a wide spot in the dirt road.

"This is where you must meet me. I'll be here in two hours."

He climbed down from the truck. Jake and Chanti joined him, carrying their weapons, but leaving the blankets in the cab.

Balthazar pointed at a faint trail between two large trees.

"Head off there. Go west. You'll come to a ridge. That's the half-way point. Another kilometer beyond that is a rocky cliff side. The cave is there. Head for the highest point on the cliff and the cave is almost directly under it. The entrance is hidden by a grove of thorny trees that are difficult to get through. You can't see the opening until you're practically on top of it. There are only a total of six men in the group. If you're lucky, they won't all be there. Any questions?"

"See you in a couple hours," Jake said.

Chanti lifted her hand in parting and they struck out straight between the two trees. The forest wasn't as thick as the jungles they were used to and they jogged to the ridge. Before they passed over it, Chanti paused and cut up a stout hardwood tree limb into two three-foot clubs. Something thrashed through the thick brush nearby. Wheeling, Jake glimpsed the back end of a deer as it vanished.

After crossing the ridge, the cliff side became visible and they kept jogging toward the high point.

Half a kilometer from the thick grove of trees, they slowed to a walk and glided through the forest like two phantoms. No sound. They threaded their way through the thorn trees and inched up to a tiny clearing.

Jake parted thorny shrubs and exposed the entrance to the cave. Both crawled closer to the small opening, where a man squatted on his haunches, eyes closed, back leaning against the rocks. He supported himself with his rifle. The man made an easy target, but they had already decided not to kill anyone.

The guard shuddered as if he sensed danger.

Jake crept up to the kidnapper and slammed the wooden club into the side of his head. He toppled over and didn't move. Jake picked up the man's rifle and ejected the clip and the cartridge in the breech. He threw the rifle into the trees and the ammunition in the opposite direction.

Jake's rage shot a strong flow of energy through him. Any doubts disappeared.

Watch out, Zapatistas. Here we come.

Chanti slipped through the entrance. Jake followed a step behind. His heart beat faster.

They each stepped to opposite sides of the doorway to remain invisible.

A large, cold grotto confronted them. Two smaller spaces branched off the rear of the room. Between the two, a fire blazed. Cots lined the walls of the small rooms. Two men sat at a wooden table on wooden benches off to the left. A kerosene lantern lit the table so they could see their cards. Three more human forms lay on cots in the rear left hand room.

Wouldn't you know it! All six are here. Oh, well. Five to go.

Jake caught his breath. His parents sat on two cots in the right hand room. Both wore metal shackles on their wrists and ankles. They faced each other, holding hands. Jake's heart swelled. His adrenaline spiked.

Jake drifted along the wall to the left.

Chanti slipped to the right.

They skirted the bundles of weapons, blankets, sacks of rice, lentils, dried vegetables and nuts stacked everywhere.

Neither card player saw past the umbrella of light cast by the dim lantern.

Jake and Chanti glided into the light and struck with their clubs. Crack, crack. Almost an echo. The unconscious men slumped to the cavern floor.

One of the sleeping kidnappers rolled over and sat up.

Jake dashed toward him like a quarter horse blasting out of the gate. Chanti kept pace with him.

The man's mouth dropped open as Jake charged him, arm lifted with his club.

"Aargh!" he screamed.

At the same time, Chanti closed in on the other two. Both of them sat up.

The screamer reached for his rifle. He lifted it, finger finding the trigger.

Jake's right hand slashed the club down across the rifle. The stroke mangled the man's left hand wrapped around the forestock.

The Zapatista shrieked like a banshee. The weapon clattered to the stony floor.

Chanti hacked with her club, nailing one man on top of his head. His knees buckled and he dropped to the floor like discarded clothing. His eyes bulged and a scream stuck in his throat.

Jake whirled and his club streaked for the last man's head. Chanti's slammed into it at the same time. He dropped like a stone.

Jake wheeled back to the first one and chopped the club down on his head.

"Hah! Lucky again!" Jake laughed.

"True enough, El Tuerto," Chanti chuckled.

Jake slipped around the corner to find his parents, eleven days after his attempted kidnapping.

"Mom, Dad. Are you okay. Did they hurt you?"

Both stood, but couldn't approach him because of the shackles.

"Oh, Jake," his mom said. "How in the world did you find us?"

Jake hugged her. She clung to him and kissed his cheek several times. His dad made it a group hug. Tears ran down the cheeks of all three.

Jake released his dad and turned toward Chanti.

"Mom, Dad, this is Chanti. She saved me and now she's saved you."

"Oh, Chanti. I'm so happy to meet you," Jake's mom said.

"Likewise. Thank you," Jake's dad said.

"A pleasure to meet you both. Sorry it took so long."

"I guess we need to find a key for these shackles. Do you know which man has it?" Jake said.

Jake's dad said, "The tallest man had it in his pocket."

"We'll be right back. We need to tie them up, too."

Jake and Chanti vanished around the corner. Jake pulled a coil of rope from his backpack. I'm going to drag the guard in from outside. Will you cut this into sizes we can tie them all up with, please?"

"Sure."

Jake jogged to the entrance and stepped outside. He grasped the still unconscious man by the ankles and dragged him inside to the table. Working together, they soon bound all six securely, wrists and ankles drawn up behind their backs. Several might have concussions, but all still lived.

"I found the keys," Chanti held up a half dozen on a ring. She handed them to Jake.

"Let's get them loose."

Jake took several giant steps to his parents. Kneeling down, he tried two before he found the right key. He unshackled their ankles first, then their wrists.

His mom threw her arms around him.

"Oh, Jake. I rarely ever get scared, but I was here. They didn't abuse us, but their attitude frightened me. Where's Chanti? She's adorable. Are you two in love?"

Jake glanced over his shoulder. Chanti had disappeared.

"I'll look. Come on outside."

Jake strode to the opening and through it. Chanti leaned against the cliff side. A single tear ran down her face. Jake smiled and took a step toward her. She swerved to stay an arm's length from him.

"I'm feeling sorry for myself, seeing you three together. And my mom and dad are gone. Even Ba lam's gone and he's been with me since they died."

She's backing out. I can't lose her now.

Her emptiness left him with a physical ache in his chest.

"Will you come to New Mexico with us? You'll never be more welcome anywhere."

Chanti turned to look him in the eyes and stepped close. She put her arms around him and pinned him against the rock wall. He couldn't move and couldn't speak and didn't want to.

"Aren't you going to kiss me?" she said.

Author's Note

I've enjoyed action/adventure for as long as I can remember, either through personal involvement or reading about it in books like this one.

While living part-time in Mexico, I had the good fortune to meet Dimitar Krustev, a Bulgarian born artist living in the expat community, Ajijic, on the shores of Lake Chapala. In the 1960s, Krustev ventured into Chiapas where he lived for many months with the Lacandon Indians before the jungles began to disappear. His tales of adventure and danger inspired me to write VANISHED. After all, what better location to set an action thriller than the jungle with so many deadly creatures to encounter.

I alluded to many of the jungle's changes since Krustev's time there, but certain liberties have been taken in portraying the lives of the Lacandons. The towns are real, but the characters are entirely fictitious.

For more information about my work and other novels, visit my website at www.HankBarone.com.

Please read on for chapter one of
my new novel, BETRAYED,
available soon!

BETRAYED

1

Lori fired up the diesel, backed off the dock and took a quick swing through the narrow passage. Boats of all types crowded the Spanish Town marina. Not much room was left to maneuver.

She spun the wheel to make a sharp right turn.

A loud "thunk" boomed, then a jolt through the helm tightened her white-knuckled grip.

The boat failed to turn.

Yang Soon lunged straight for a houseboat docked ahead.

She slammed the engine into reverse.

Too late. The forward thrust carried the 36-foot sailboat straight ahead. It was like trying to stop a car sliding toward a tree on black ice.

A loud splintering followed a thundering crack. *Yang Soon's* sleek bow sliced into the wall and roof of the houseboat's living room, well above the water line, much the same as a wrecking ball smashed through an old building.

The impact jolted her like someone punched her chest with a giant fist. Her eyes bugged out. Her breathing came in deep gulps.

Lori leaned out of the cockpit and looked down to see a man and woman clad in shorts and t-shirts staring up from their chairs, mouths agape. The bow ground to a halt ten feet in front of them. The couple dropped the books they had been reading and toppled from their chairs, away from the prow.

The boat lurched, the motor coughed and died. Lori slumped, chin sagging to her chest.

I can't believe it. Dad'd sure be proud of me now. My first try without his guidance and I wreck two boats.

She sucked in a deep breath and stood straight. "Are you all right?" she called down.

"I'm okay," came a deep, angry voice. "You, Midge?"

"Fine, John. Scraped knee, that's all." She looked at Lori. "What in the world happened, dear? Scared me to death."

"Steering cable snapped while I was turning. Couldn't stop in time. I've made that turn dozens of times before. I'm so sorry. I'll get your boat fixed. Can you call Bob at the marina's office? I can't back out of here without the helm. I'd probably hit something else."

"Look at this mess. I've been in a car accident, but never a boat wreck when I'm tied up at the dock," John snarled.

"Aren't you Matt Wagner's daughter, Lori?" asked Midge.

"Yes, Ma'am."

"How old're you?" John asked, still angry.

"Nineteen."

"We're very sorry for your loss, Lori. Such a shock. Your dad always seemed so indestructible, and only 44 years old," Midge said.

Lori's eyes teared up. "Thank you," she said. Lori could see him now - not murdered, lying in a casket as he had arrived home - but the way he was when she was a child. At six feet four inches and 225 pounds, he had seemed like a giant, but he had always been so gentle. Tears streamed from her ebony eyes.

"I'm Midge Edelson and this is my husband, John."

"Bob will solve our problem shortly," John griped.

It's time to suck it up and face the music. Gotta go down there.

Lori hung onto a line from her boat and dropped down to the houseboat's deck. "May I use your phone to call my Uncle Jack? He lives here, on island." She said.

"Are you talking about Jack Dolan?" John said. "A very strange man. I heard you don't want to mess with him. His picture's in the dictionary right there next to the word nightmare." He paused as Midge elbowed him. "Sorry. I shouldn't have said that."

"It's okay. Dad said he's a tortured soul who doesn't fit a familiar mold and it worries people. He's not really my uncle, but Dad and Mom have always looked out for him. Now there's only me. I don't know him too well, because I've spent most of my time in New Mexico and he spends his time at our place here in the British Virgin Islands on Virgin Gorda. When I am here, it's usually to go sailing and he doesn't like boats."

Taking the proffered cell phone from John with a shaky hand, Lori punched in her uncle's number.

I hope this is one of Jack's good days and he answers the phone.

Two nights ago she had gotten to know him better. Feeling downhearted that Matt had died, he told her a little about his past. In answer to her question about why he sometimes spent days at a time in his apartment without venturing outside, he said, "Sometimes I'm just too messed up to be with people. I'm probably half crazy and I'm dangerous. Not a night goes by I don't have to dope myself up to sleep, only to have horrible dreams anyway. When I feel really over the edge, I know better than to go out."

"Did you meet Dad in the Marines?"

"No. We met after I was discharged. I'm twenty years older than your dad was. He'd been through some of the same things I had. He and your mom, Sue, were the only two people who ever helped me."

"You're from the States. How come you've never visited us in New Mexico?" Lori asked.

"When I enlisted, I already had a police record and did some time. I got in trouble when I went back to the states after Vietnam. All the US taught me was to kill. I was considered one thing, a 'kill' machine. The government made me promise to not rob, kill or molest and they pay me to stay out of the US. I have no country and I'm glad of it because they're all so screwed up they make me puke."

Jack Dolan answered the phone on the tenth ring, sidetracking Lori from her thoughts.

"Uncle Jack? Lori."

"I thought you'd be gone by now."

"I know. I was supposed to be, but I had an accident."

"Are you hurt?"

"No. I'm okay, but I rammed *Yang Soon* into a houseboat. The steering cable broke. Can you come to the marina?"

"Sure. Be there soon. If my car starts."

"Thanks, Uncle Jack. You can't miss *Yang Soon* jammed into the houseboat. See you then." Lori hung up and handed the phone back to John.

"I'd better get my insurance papers. Be right back," Lori scampered up the line to her boat. Thousands of workouts gave her no feeling of haste. Each motion flowed into the next.

In moments she slipped back down with a packet of papers.

"Where were you headed?" asked Midge.

"I was going to Dominica to scatter Dad's ashes. He always loved that Caribbean island the most."

The marina owner, Bob Douglas, stuck his head in the doorway.

"Hello, John, Midge, Lori. We'll get this mess straightened out in no time. We'll put a temporary cover over the houseboat's damaged area after we get *Yang Soon* out of here and back to her own slip. I know Matt had insurance, Lori. It looks like you have the papers there. You want me to take care of this?"

"Yes, please, Bob. I don't know how to handle it." Lori's voice shook as she explained what had happened.

"Okay. You'll have to sign some papers later. Glad nobody got hurt. Both boats will be fixed soon. Midge and John, you might want to check into a hotel until the repairs are made. Lori, it'll probably be tomorrow before yours is fixed. I'll have them touch up the bow, too. Can you get home all right?"

"Sure. My Uncle Jack is coming."

"How is Jack? Haven't seen him around for a while."

"Same old Uncle Jack," Lori said. She faced John and Midge, "We can take you to a hotel."

"Thanks, dear, but we'll probably stick around until the repairmen get here," Midge said.

"You've both been very kind to take this so well. I'm so sorry this happened. Call me if there's anything I can do." Lori turned to the marina owner. "Bob, okay if I leave my stuff aboard?"

"Sure, Lori. No problem. I'll lock it up. Keys in the ignition?"

"Yep. I'll be down later, or more likely, tomorrow morning."

Jack, a rugged six-feet-two-inch man with a big frame, stepped onto the houseboat's deck. Everyone turned when the boat dipped. He looked a little ragged, but he had not been a movie star to begin with.

As Lori walked to greet him, she marveled that the contrast between the two of them was so obvious, like life and death. She had never realized how pale he was, but in the bright sunlight it was easy to see.

Both his face and body appeared somewhat bloated. Nondescript except for his wide-brimmed black hat and black clothes, he limped as he plodded to the doorway. The black outfit set off his white, pony-tailed hair, white mustache and pasty skin. The only thing colorful about Jack was his multihued hatband with a dart shoved in it. She recalled her dad telling her it was a poisoned dart.

Lori glanced down at her flawless, honeyed skin, from her Korean mother, which made her look much darker than she was when she approached him. Having inherited her size from her dad, she stood only three inches shorter than Jack.

"Uncle Jack. Thanks for coming." She smiled and hugged him. "I've sure made a mess of things. John and Midge, this is Jack Dolan."

Jack gave a small wave and the others nodded.

Lori led Jack from the houseboat to the dock, explaining all that had happened. They climbed into Jack's dented 1980 Toyota Land Cruiser.

"I don't know why, but I'm hungry. Can we stop somewhere?" Lori said.

"Sure. How about the No Scum Allowed Saloon. They have good food."

"Great."

Jack drove them to the tavern.

Along the way, he pointed out a black Volvo following them. It made every turn he did.

"Lori, you ever seen that car behind us?"

"No. Is it following us?"

"Seems to be."

The saloon was painted eye-catching colors and sporting a thatched roof. A white sign hung at a 45-degree angle beside the door. In black print, it read No Scum Allowed. The establishment originally bore the name Spanish Town Saloon, but for years had been called what the sign said.

The car behind sped past them as Jack parked. Lori couldn't see through its dark, tinted windows.

Lori and Jack sat at a table in the middle of the main room decorated with fishnets, hundreds of business cards stapled to the walls amidst advertisements for Pusser's Rum and Red Stripe Beer, and an odd abundance of panties and bras of all sizes and colors hanging from the ceiling. At the bar, three men drank, doubled over with laughter and drank again. Happy hour was a huge success. The tallest of the three moved the hands of the wall clock back and extended Happy Hour a full 15 minutes before his plot was discovered.

Another, wearing a blue polo shirt, khaki shorts, scuffed Topsiders with a blue baseball cap pushed back on his head, acted the part of a confident yachtsman. A large paunch suggested there had been many days like this one; wild partying, drinking with near strangers, swapping lies, letting go.

"Watch those guys," Jack said. "There's going to be trouble."

The yachtsman threw back another double.

"I don't guess he'll be standing much longer," Lori said.

The man flicked his lighter and ignited a mouthful of rum that spewed flames into the air toward the roof. The dry, thatched roof.

www.ingramcontent.com/pod-product-compliance
Lightning Source LLC
Chambersburg PA
CBHW050505260626
47157CB00004B/1198